Prelude

DRESDAN COVEN

AMBER ELLA MONROE

Copyright © 2015 Amber Ella Monroe
Published by Obsidian Gem Publishing LLC

http://amberellabooks.com

ISBN-13: 978-1517525996
ISBN-10: 1517525993

This is a work of fiction. The characters, places, incidents, and dialogues in this book are of the author's imagination and are not to be construed as real. Any resemblance to actual events or person, living or dead, is completely coincidental.

All rights reserved. No part of this publication may be reproduced, stored in a retrieval system, or transmitted in any form or by any means, electronic, mechanical, recording or otherwise, without the prior written permission of the author.

Printed in the U.S.A.

OTHER PARANORMAL ROMANCE TITLES

AMBER ELLA MONROE
AMBRIELLE KIRK

BLOOD LEGENDS
The Protector

CAEDMON WOLVES
Wolf's Haven
Wolf's Promise
Wolf's Touch
Caedmon Wolves Volume One
Wolf's Desire
Wolf's Strength
Wolf's Honor
Caedmon Wolves Volume Two

DRESDAN COVEN
Prelude
Donor
Requiem

WOLF IN EXILE

Captured

Unchained

Ascend

Reclaimed

Wolf in Exile: The Complete Edition

ASPEN VALLEY PACK (BAD BOYS)

Shifter Untamed

If you enjoy romance with an edgier side, subscribe to Amber Ella's newsletter, http://smarturl.it/amberellas-list, and be one of the first to be notified of new releases, current contests, giveaways, and book-related news.

For paranormal romance novels, visit Amber Ella Monroe on the web at http://amberellabooks.com

For contemporary romance novels, visit Ambrielle Kirk on the web at http://booksbyambrielle.com

STORY SUMMARY

When District 5 discovers that vampire tracker Elaina, one of their best employees, has taken sides with the very same beings they hunt down, her leaders put out a bounty on her—payable to anyone for her live capture. Her lover, Vicq, will do anything to prevent losing Elaina, even if it means risking his own existence. But when the Master vampire of the Dresdan Court learns of Vicq's dealings with a slayer, he is sentenced to death. When their location is compromised, the countdown begins in the fight for their lives.

PROLOGUE

"Vida o muerte?"

"What?" the dying man croaked, confusion marking his face.

"Life or death? Which do you choose?"

Vicq's Maker had given him this choice long ago. Not one ounce of hesitation consumed him as he extended the same options to the infected and wounded man lying on his back on the pavement, coughing up blood and struggling to stay alive.

The fact that a Dresdan had drained a human within a few short mildes of his coven alarmed him. When Vicq had set up his coven near the foothills of the Black Mountains, the territory had been vacant of any vampires. Was Master Russo getting close to finding his sanctuary? Had he sent another army of Dresdan Soldiers to track him down? Or was it mere coincidence that this man was left here to die?

"I'm already dying, aren't I?" the man asked, sputtering up blood.

"You've been drained by a vampire—a Dresdan. *Sí*...eventually you will."

"Well, why don't you finish me then, vamp?" he spat. "I'm too weak to move, and the sun has burned me to a crisp. Put me out of my misery...please."

"You're alive because you were infected with Dresdan blood before you were drained. What did you do? Try to square off with one of us?"

"Yes," he hissed between clenched teeth. "I didn't know he was a dirty, stinking vamp."

Vicq shook his head and tapped the roof of his mouth with his tongue. "Careful. It's a miracle that you still speak. Based on the amount of blood dried up around you and your current state, I don't expect you to live more than a half hour. If you're not dead by then, the sun rises again in five hours, and that'll surely kill you. Whoever drained you and left you for dead wanted your passing to be slow. You can wait

Prelude

just another half an hour for death, can't you?"

The man grumbled but couldn't lash out due to his weakened state.

Vicq continued to speak, "To the north, there're mountains. To the west, more mountains. To the east, we have valleys. You're out in the middle of nowhere here, and miles from any hospital." Vicq waved his arm to illustrate the landfill just a few yards behind him. "What's a human doing out here, anyway?"

"I was...delivering a car. A Ferrari. Top of the line. The vamp betrayed me. He took the car and left me."

"You don't have much blood left. Decide quickly. I can give you more time, but, of course, you'll be forever changed."

"You're one of them. One of those bloodsuckers who did this to me. I don't know if I can trust you."

"When I feed from humans, I don't get messy."

"If..." The man coughed. "If I take your blood, will I become like you?"

Vicq's intuition told him that the man was worth

saving or turning. And he had learned long ago that listening to his initial hunches was beneficial.

"Depends... Life or death?"

Creating a vampire and then leaving him alone to fend for himself was against the Dresdan code.

"Life, of course."

Vicq lifted the injured man, bringing him to a sitting position. He brought his wrist to his fangs, split his vein, and offered the man his arm. "Drink, but not too much. You might feel a little drowsy afterward. There's a motel five miles up the road from here. I'll get you there to recover after this, but I suggest you stay inside for at least three days."

"Will I be normal again?"

"What do you think? You've been bitten by Dresdan. Enough with the questions, human. You won't be the same, but you won't be a vampire either."

"Why should I trust you?"

"You shouldn't."

The man looked at him apprehensively. "What

Prelude

will I owe you?"

"When I'm in need of a car, I'll come to you."

He didn't miss the light sparkle of hope in the man's eyes.

"Cómo se llama?" Vicq asked.

"Emory," the man whispered. His lips had turned ashen white and his eyes virtually soulless as he struggled to hold on to what little life force was left in him.

"When you've had enough of being a human on the edge of insanity with a taste for blood instead of food, and you're ready to cross over, remember my name. *Vicq*."

The man cupped Vicq's wrist in his hands and tipped it to his lips.

He'd chosen life. Vicq wasn't surprised. Most any human would choose their life over uncertain death.

Most any human...but not him.

Life or death.

When Vicq had been given the choice by his Maker

Amber Ella Monroe

over sixty years ago, he'd chosen death because life, as it was back then, was both uncertain and unjust.

CHAPTER ONE

───── ❖ ─────

Two and a half months later...

Elaina Arakelian turned her wrist over and glanced at the time on her watch again. 8:01AM. She had less than an hour to reach the District 5 base for scheduled training, yet all the tables at The Pancake Hut were occupied. The eatery was busy, as was expected during the breakfast rush. It was the only diner within a fifteen-mile radius of the base. This place had been here for years, even before the District set up shop, yet they refused to add takeout service. She was hungry and extremely low on fuel. So, she'd wait. From here, it would only take her fifteen minutes to reach base. If she timed it just right, she could get there on time.

When Elaina looked up again, she noticed that many other District 5 members were here to grab breakfast before training started. Among them were full-fledged trackers—just like her—and recruits. She wasn't on a first-name basis with any of them—yet. Her priorities were simple. Train, complete assignments, and collect her paycheck and monthly stipend. Upon recruitment, they'd been told not to use their legal names. They weren't allowed to hold on to any fragments of their past lives. They were basically dead to the rest of the world. They'd pledged their life to the mission. Even in death, they would all become the property of District 5.

It was too early in Elaina's contract to forget her family and friends. She didn't know that she would *ever* forget them, but it was her duty now to remain at a distance and protect from the shadows. She still had many memories. Her memories were her own and no one else's. Nobody could take that from her. But that didn't change the fact that she was still bound to District 5's mission.

"Ma'am?"

Elaina's attention shifted to the server, standing to the right of her.

Prelude

"We have a seat for one," the server continued.

She followed the server to an empty stool near the serving bar. Three cooks manned their individual stations directly in front of her. They seemed to be working quickly despite the number of order tickets the waitresses threw at them.

Eggs were being cooked on the griddle, sunny-side up. Sausage and bacon sizzled. Steam floated up from the pancake tray. This was the closest she'd get to a home-cooked meal.

Elaina looked down at her watch again just as a waitress approached her. 8:07AM. From the looks of it, she'd have just enough time to pig out. She ordered the breakfast platter that was chock-full of protein. She'd need it. This was the last training session of the season for trackers. If she passed with flying colors, the District 5 heads would be more likely to hand her an assignment worthy of her skills.

For the past few months, all she'd been doing was knocking off the occasional rogue or wayward vampire. Those assignments were getting too easy for her.

She was getting bored...and curious about the other, inner workings of the District—an organization whose mission was to prolong the existence of mankind by capturing, destroying, and salvaging vampires.

Elaina worked from the shadows at night and trained and rested during the day. Whenever she or one of her colleagues knocked off a rogue vampire, they were ordered to collect the blood. In very rare cases, if they could capture one, they were ordered to bring it to the labs. The District 5 lab techs were interested in vampire blood the most. The older and more powerful the vampire, the better.

To date, there had been under two dozen accounts of vampires being held captive and taken in. Likewise, there had been several dozen accounts of District 5 recruits and trackers being murdered by vampires while on assignment. It was a dangerous job...but Elaina was being paid to do it. She didn't get a thrill from killing vampires, but she did gain a sense of achievement from killing vampires who slaughtered humans mercilessly and without reason.

Prelude

Of course, there were vampires who slipped out at night, fed, and kept their donors alive, but those numbers were small in comparison to the rogues who killed to feed. During training, recruits were told to presume that if a vampire revealed itself, he or she was there to kill. Elaina didn't need to test that theory. Even though she had sacrificed her life to become a member of the District, she wanted to live.

However, she wanted to be more than the recruit who took orders and followed her superiors without asking questions. One day, she wanted to be a leader who gave orders. She wanted to make a difference, and she wanted to stand for something greater than she could ever imagine.

Her father always told her, "Be careful what you crave. Sometimes, your cravings can turn out to be your worst nightmare."

Other than the occasional bruise to her ego after losing a fight or two or letting a rogue vampire get away, she hadn't experienced any nightmares. Yet. Something told her that she should still heed her father's warnings; but so far, she hadn't done so. Some of her cravings were just too persistent. Sooner or later, Elaina would find out that one relentless craving could change her life forever.

CHAPTER TWO

———— ❖ ————

"I can see that District heads are still hiring and promoting girls 'round here."

The statement came from Danny, a colleague in Elaina's unit. He was more than a colleague, actually. He'd recently been selected as the leader of her work unit. She may be required to follow his orders, but she certainly wasn't keen on putting up with his bullshit comments.

Elaina lowered the chilled bottle of water she was chugging down and gave him a quick glance. He grinned smugly and used the hand towel around his thick neck to wipe sweat from his face.

"I'm not your optometrist. I'm not the one you need to convince that you can see," she said and moved to the other side of the courtyard.

Her unit was only five minutes into a break after two and a half hours of grueling physical maintenance drills. Danny had followed her, but her idea of rest didn't include talking to a guy she couldn't stand.

"Why'd you walk off like that? Can't I have a chat with you?" he asked.

"Just because we're in the same unit and you've been assigned as my superior, doesn't mean that I want to engage in small talk with you."

Danny shrugged. "Why not? If we're going to be working together for the next few months on assignments, you've gotta learn to love my influence around here. Especially now that you've been promoted as next in line *under* me."

"Influence?" She almost laughed. "I don't have to like the people that I work with, and that includes you."

"Girl, who's fucking you the wrong way for you to carry such an attitude day in and day out?" he asked.

"You keep calling me *girl*, but does it bother you that I've beaten every one of your scores since we started training together?"

Prelude

Danny's grin disappeared. "It doesn't matter. You're still *under* me, and you'll always be. You've beaten my training stats but when we're in the real world, fighting those vamps, can you apply the same skills, girl? Or will you watch from the sidelines as your partners take them out? Those cold-hearted scumbags don't have a taste for tits and ass like half of these men out here who've been distracted by the women training beside them do. Pretty women like you, flaunting your assets all over the training field. The vamps are interested in blood. They kill to drink and nothing distracts hunger."

"You're so sure of yourself," she shot back. "It also sounds like you're frustrated because you don't get laid at all. Too bad. But if you want to put your money where your mouth is, our next session includes hand-to-hand combat. I've been yearning for something bigger and meatier to punch in the face, and these women don't measure up."

Danny scoffed. "You're delusional."

"Scared?" she taunted.

"D-33!" One of the drill instructors yelled her number from across the field.

Without another word, she turned and jogged over to him to acknowledge her presence. "Here."

"Injection time. Report to Level E, Station B1."

As part of her employment contract with District 5, Elaina was required to receive a drug injection on a periodic basis to ward off vampire infection. Humans had been known to die after coming in contact with vampire blood, which was said to be poisonous to humans if not taken directly from a vein.

One of the missions Elaina was bound to undertake was to fight and execute vampires, so coming in contact with their blood was likely. During her unit's training period, they'd been presented with numerous accounts of District 5 trackers perishing after failing to undergo the injections.

On her way to Level E, Elaina walked slowly through the corridors. Recruiters and trackers weren't given many opportunities to explore the entire District

Prelude

headquarters, which was at least two football fields long and had seven levels, two of which were underground. The underground levels were completely off limits to unauthorized staff, mostly because they contained captured vampires, both dead and alive. Well,...they were all dead. But the vampires that had expired were kept on ice for further testing.

The other levels of District 5 required controlled access, but the District operations were so complex that Elaina had yet to uncover all of the inner workings. She was a vampire tracker, and her duties never crossed over to the business or operations side of the organization. She was hired on purely to assist with tactics. But what person wouldn't be grossly interested in other areas of an organization they'd signed their life over to?

The overall mission made sense: Ensure human continuity. And she didn't want to die. Not by a vampire's hand, anyway. If vampires took over, human downfall would be eminent. But there were politics in the ongoing structure that warranted her attention.

She passed one of the labs that kept live humans. LBs or Live Bodies were what she'd heard these people referred to as. Basically, they were humans who'd given up their bodies in the name of scientific research. More often than not, the humans were sick or had terminal illnesses, but there were a few accounts of healthy individuals agreeing to have tests performed on them.

The shades weren't drawn closed in one of the labs, and she caught a glimpse of a middle-aged man sitting on a metal operating table. He was stark naked and devoid of all body hair. A nurse pulled a machine up beside the table and took his blood pressure reading. The middle-aged man wasn't the only subject in the room. There was at least a handful more being monitored by the nursing staff.

The man caught her stare through the glass. He didn't look happy. His expression was cold and unfeeling.

Elaina was loyal to the mission, but she often wondered if she would acquiesce if it came down to

Prelude

her being sent to labs for testing in that manner. Her passion was in tactics, so she knew without a doubt that becoming a lab rat wasn't a desirable choice for her.

There was already a staff member waiting for her when Elaina arrived at Station B1.

"D-33?" the young woman asked. She looked to be in her mid to late twenties.

After confirming her identity, Elaina sat down in the hard metal chair and placed her arm on the rest. She'd gotten the injections many times before, mostly when there was a big assignment coming up. It was never a surprise anymore. In a couple days, she would probably get another email with an assignment order attached to it.

"It says here that this will be your last monitored injection. Today, you will go home with your own kit. Do you understand how to administer the injections yourself?"

"I do."

The woman handed her the elastic strip and a needle filled with clear blue liquid. "Go ahead, D-33. Let's see what you can do."

In less than a minute, Elaina had found a vein and injected the serum.

"Do you understand when the injections need to happen?" the tech asked.

"Right before every assignment."

The woman nodded and scribbled on her clipboard. "I need you to sign here, here, and here, indicating that you will not misuse, under use, or over use the injections." She pointed to three read X's on the page. "They will be replenished as assignments are given. You agree by acknowledging you were informed."

Elaina grabbed the fountain pen and wrote her new alias: D-33.

Just as Elaina was about to exit through the double doors, a loud boom echoed from the other side of the space. She spun around to see two male staff members hauling a screaming girl into the room. The high-pitched squeals were unnerving. The girl managed to

Prelude

claw one of the male staff across the face, cutting into the skin and drawing blood. The screaming girl broke free, and yet another man joined in to drag her farther into the room.

Elaina was so shocked that her feet were rooted to the floor as she processed the scene before her.

"Let me go," the girl screamed.

"She's infected! Get her on the table and in the straps!" someone yelled.

The girl's gaze was wild with fear and filled with something else. Her eyes were shaded with a red filter, something that only happened when an individual came in contact with vampire blood. Dresdan blood to be exact. The whites of their eyes turned a muted red when they were riding high on aggression.

The girl let out another blood-curdling scream that could have shattered the glass in the room. She bared her teeth and hissed, and her eyes glossed over as if she were possessed.

They managed to slam her down on a hard metal table where she flopped about until all of her limbs plus her midsection were strapped tightly to the slab.

"The infection has set in for far too long. She's gone. We're going to have to turn her over to Level B."

Level B. It was where the infected staff was placed in small observation rooms. Many of them perished there. Hardly any of them crossed over or changed while in that state.

"D-33! Exit the room!" the young woman who had injected Elaina earlier ordered.

Elaina could not tear her eyes away from the sight of the girl. Infected and crazed out of her mind, but yet she looked so young and innocent. What had happened to her?

One of the straps on the table popped as the girl fought against her bonds. She began to choke on her own blood, puddles of it pouring out of her mouth and onto the lab floor.

"Blood! We need blood!" one of the male staffed yelled.

"D-33! Out!"

Prelude

Elaina tore her eyes away from the sight and pushed the double doors open. Her legs shook as she quickened her pace, and before long, she was running down the corridors back to the training fields.

When she reached the outside again, she exhaled violently and doubled over in exertion.

"Oh my gosh," she whispered softly to herself. She prayed the girl received help. No one should have to go through that.

But in her mind, Elaina somehow knew it was too late for the girl.

There was no known cure for the infection. There was only prevention. There was no going back now. The young girl's death was imminent.

CHAPTER THREE

Just as Elaina had expected, she received a text alert that evening. The message instructed her that the details of the night's assignment had been emailed to her. After training class had ended, her plan was to sleep in until her real shift began, but as soon as she drifted off, memories of the infected girl's screams came back to her.

The insides of her mouth were now raw from biting her lips in worry and aggravation over what happened on Level E inside Station B. What had happened to the girl?

The fear that had been instilled in all District 5 contractors and employees was if they didn't take the injections as supplied and prescribed, then the same fate might await them.

Only a small percentage of the human population could sustain life with a vampire infection. One of

D5's missions was to find out how to identify those people, and talk them into willingly supplying their DNA or giving access to their bodies in the name of scientific research. There had been many leads since the research project began—and even before Elaina signed her employment contract—but as soon as the key researchers insisted they had something, the individual would turn up missing.

The only way to determine if someone could actually live with a vampire infection was to let him or her become infected.

If the person turned out like the girl in the labs, then it ultimately meant death. But what D5 was trying to obtain was a person capable of contracting the vampire infection without dying. A person that could become a hybrid, a cross between a human and a vampire. A breed that would stand up for humans to prevent bloodsuckers from taking over the world.

Elaina rose from the hammock on her patio, took one last look at the tops of the city buildings and towers below her, and walked through the sliding glass doors

Prelude

to enter her condo. D5 paid the room and board for all contractors, but trackers were required to use D5 housing. The best thing about the job was probably the downtime, free room and board, and the fact that she didn't have to cook, clean, or do any of the things she'd had to do when she had her own apartment. The condo she lived in was quite elaborate. Top of the line structure. Valet parking, courteous staff, and thorough cleaning services. She had nothing to complain about here.

Her laptop was already open on her bar. She used her thumbprint to power it on and entered a series of passcodes to get into her email.

"Vampire crew sighting in the area 25 miles north of your location in the vicinity of Heagert Community College where 2 students were murdered while walking home from a party...witness confirmed 3 vampire entities carrying the bodies away and they were found in a remote field drained and dead within hours by campus security....vampire attacks have been attempted nightly with the same description of

the suspects: 3 deadly vampires. 6PM campus curfew in effect. Risk level: 7/10 - Unit Members Assigned: D-209, D-33, D-0008, D-57. Assignment: Track and Execute. You have 24 hours from midnight to complete this assignment."

Elaina's last track and execute assignment—which she and her unit had successfully completed—had been just three nights ago. A risk level seven wasn't all that bad. It probably meant the vampires were young; not the older, stronger ones that the District wished to get their hands on to study and take blood from so that they could farm a hybrid in the labs.

Her highest risk level ever had been an eight, where she and six other D5 trackers were sent to take out rogue vampires responsible for the murders of five families, all in one neighborhood. Fledgling and rogue vampires usually rolled in cliques. They needed numbers where they lacked in strength because they weren't as strong as a full-fledged Dresdan. Her unit had found the slumbering place of each one and then set fire to them during the day. Fire weakened

Prelude

vampires just like UV light. Concentrating the fire to one area had weakened them beyond reason, stripping their strength. The seals to their coffins had broken open, exposing them to the sun. Since her unit had the upper hand, two or three shots to the head had ensured an instant kill.

Elaina peeled out of her pajamas and pulled her work attire from the closet. A black leather jumpsuit that she wore because it allowed free and quick movement. She owned exactly five jumpsuits. No pastel colors were allowed. Light colors attracted vampires the most. Not that she was interested in wearing pink and yellow dresses to a vampire slaying anyway.

She tugged on her boots, strapped them up, and then wrapped her thick mane of hair into a tight bun against the back of her head. After grabbing her tote bag of weapons, she pulled the door closed behind her and took twelve flights of stairs down to the lobby to meet the other three members of her work unit for tonight.

Danny, who was known as D-209, pushed off a wall near the door when she came down. D-0008 and D-57, both males, had just walked off the elevators.

D-209 grinned. "Ready for some fun?"

D-0008 cracked a smile, gnawing on chewing gum. He ordered boxes of it every week and had them shipped directly to the front desk. A different flavor for every day. "Lead the way, Boss."

CHAPTER FOUR

Elaina and her crew caught the gang of rogue vampires in the act not too far from campus. It was easy to scout out the bloodsucking murderers. All they had to do was follow their instincts, which led them to a frat party. The six o'clock curfew didn't extend off campus, so, of course, the off-site partygoers didn't heed the warnings.

As the music blasted from the open windows of the two-story mansion that housed about a dozen frat boys during the semester, rogue vampires were in the process of sucking their victims dry. It was possible that no one heard their screams or even noticed they were gone. By the amount of noise coming from the interior, there looked to be a good amount of partiers crowded inside.

Elaina made out the three vampires feeding on a human male and female through her riflescope. By their state of half-dress, she figured they'd been making out before the rogues struck. How unfortunate.

Her post was on the roof of an adjacent, unoccupied mansion. The other three members of her unit were on the ground, surrounding the vampire suspects in an attempt to prevent escape—if they tried.

The vampires were too involved in feeding to realize they were caught and about to be shot dead. Well, dead was an understatement. Executed. Blasted from the face of the Earth.

But one wrong move from any of Elaina's crew, and they would all be busted and possibly fail their mission. The vampires could disappear at any moment, free to murder again, which would be the worst case scenario. Even worse still, however, the rogues could turn on Elaina's crew, and *they'd* become the victims.

Since her crew had been given orders to execute, the best way to do that was to strike from afar with little to no contact—which also ensured a successful kill.

Prelude

Elaina already had her assigned target in her scope before the order was given by Danny to shoot.

When she fired, her bullet hit the target clean through the head. Even though she was far away, she could tell she had a direct hit by the way the vampire's head popped back from the force of her bullet.

The other shots were fired almost simultaneously. The rogues never had a chance as each team member's aim was precisely positioned to kill. The vampires withered away next to their human victims, never really knowing what had hit them.

Elaina wished all assignments and rogue executions were this clean, but she knew that wasn't possible. The rogues were weaker than full-blooded Dresdan, especially if they were just made. And by the way these three had mindlessly attacked the college campus night after night, anyone could tell they'd been desperate for blood and too weak to prey on anything other than students.

Tonight's assignment was completed. Three murderous predators were off the streets, but, of course, there were hundreds, possibly thousands more to go.

CHAPTER FIVE

Vampires were fucking all over the goddamned club. Even in plain sight.

Vicq could sense it in the air, see it at every turn he made around a corner, and could even taste the erotic thrill in the blood exchanges being made that night.

It was an initiation night, which meant a human had recently been turned and welcomed into a coven. Besides Vicq's, there were four other covens here tonight in the bar. They had traveled from all the way across the country to get here. It was a good thing many of his coven members were strong enough and old enough that they didn't need to travel the human way. Shifting from city to city in tandem at the speed of light made the trip shorter. Of course, it never allowed time to enjoy the views.

"The weather is nice here," Eli said from across the booth. A vampiress was cuddled up beside the young scientist, her thigh draped across his lap and her fingertips tracing his bare chest.

"Of course," Vicq agreed. "It's not like the east coast."

"The chicks are hot, too," Eli said, grinning at the vampiress, who looked content to be his toy for the night.

"You southern vamps are always so straightforward," the vampiress commented. "Too bad you can't stay."

Vicq turned away as the two became intimate in the booth. Tonight was the perfect excuse to be reckless and indulge with no worries or cares, but for some reason, he wasn't up to it. He'd refused every female vampire in here that had freely offered herself for anything more than a little blood. He was glad his coven members could take part. With all of the tension back home and the rogues crossing into their territories, he was sure the party was a relief to many.

"Go get us some drinks," Eli told the female.

Prelude

She immediately got up and sauntered off through the crowd toward the bar.

When she was gone, Eli leaned over the table and said, "You're not having fun."

Vicq shrugged. "I'm not the partying type. I just like to chill and save all my energy for the thrill of the hunt."

"That's not it. You're not the type to get a thrill out of killing your own kind, not even those poor rogues. I sense you're overthinking things."

"You do?"

"Don't worry. Our sanctuary is secure. Not even a bear has made it past the barriers we set up. There's nothing that can get past without us knowing."

"I don't know about you, Eli, but I don't plan to spend my nights hidden behind the walls of that sanctuary. It doesn't help that we're hunted by both our kind and this vampire slaughtering agency."

"Ah, but that agency is mostly killing rogues, so that's less work for us. And we're not rogues."

"To a human, a vampire is a vampire. To that shady agency, a vampire is a killer. In their eyes, we are the enemy. Do you think they would hesitate to kill you because you are not a rogue?" Vicq asked.

"Good point."

"Plus, we have sound evidence that rogues aren't their only target. They've hunted Dresdan for years and have even managed to take out some of the older ones."

"But now we know what we're up against. We won't walk into their traps like the rogues or those under Russo's orders. You told us before that we have to wait for the right time to strike and shut down this vampire killing agency."

Vicq clenched his fist on the table. "Someone will pay for the ill-treatment and senseless terrorism, and for those who have perished at the hands of those bastards."

CHAPTER SIX

———— ❖ ————

Vicq and the attending members of his coven didn't leave the initiation party until well past 3AM. They were halfway across the country when they realized that they were being followed. The blood scent lingering in Vicq's wake wasn't familiar and didn't belong to any he knew. Vicq called out to his coven members where they gathered at a deserted bus station. Since they traveled in groups by trailing each other's blood scent, it took some time for everyone under his command that night to appear. Trailing was the vampire equivalent of following someone, or in this case, tracking someone down without their knowledge.

"Some of us are being trailed," Melrose said. The redheaded, former lead guitarist was one of the first to fully materialize in front of Vicq.

"I sense it, too." That could only mean that there was more than one suspect. Vicq's fangs dropped as he picked up on more unwanted presences among his coven members. *Many unwanted presences.*

Eli unfolded beside him, his eyes burning red. "And they aren't rogues..."

Rogue vampires had a slightly different blood scent than that of their Dresdan brethren. Because they killed humans when they drank, they always smelled of the bile and other unsanitary elements of their victims. Those things associated with the scent of fear right before death.

Eli was right. These were not rogues. They were Dresdan-kind.

As the last of the coven members gathered in the lot next to the bus station, a thick mist began to seep between their boots where they stood, indicating that uninvited vampires were there but had not yet materialized.

"Show yourselves," Vicq demanded.

"We don't come in peace. We're here to take all of you in." The reply echoed around them, but the source

Prelude

of it was still not identified with so many invisible intruders around them.

"In? Where?"

"Russo."

Vicq grimaced. "We've denounced ties to Russo. We're not going anywhere."

"Then we have orders to kill."

After that declaration, the rivals revealed themselves, and all hell broke loose. There were at least two Dresdan Soldiers for every one of Vicq's coven members. It was probably only by chance that they were out in the middle of nowhere at a secluded bus station. This was a sight not meant for human eyes. Vampires going head to head with other vampires. It only showed that they were threats to each other and uncontrollable. Vicq's coven members attacked with blistering force. They were all intent on not being forced to serve Master Vampire Russo, whose hatred for humanity had become so great that he failed to punish rogues who killed humans unjustly. Russo's train of thought, tactics, and missions weren't like the former Master. A Master who'd respected human life and outlined boundaries his followers followed to keep the peace. But Russo had betrayed and murdered the prior Master—a Dresdan who'd also been Vicq's Maker. And for that one simple act, Vicq would never acquiesce to Russo or refer to him as Master. Vicq had severed ties with Russo and fled the Court.

Three minutes into the group fight, and Vicq was certain more blood had been shed than what had been consumed that night. Evidence of the carnage lay in puddles in the parking lot, and on Vicq's skin and under his fingernails.

He had no taste for their blood—which no doubt would've made him stronger. The only bloodlust he favored that night was that which thirsted for destruction and the death of those who threatened his existence.

When only one of Russo's Soldiers remained alive, the night grew silent as Vicq's coven members glanced around to make sure they were all accounted for. No

Prelude

one under Vicq's leadership had perished. *Good.*

Melrose dragged the surviving Soldier and forced him to kneel in front of Vicq.

Still panting and heaving air into his lungs, Vicq wiped the blood off his hands onto the Soldier's shirt. "What is the penalty for failing to execute orders, Soldier?"

Vicq was only taunting the vampire. It was too bad he couldn't speak. Melrose had already ripped out his voice box and her nails were dug deeply into his shoulders, holding him upright.

Russo's brand was embedded in the flesh of the Solider's chest, and seeing it now through the ripped remnants of his clothes caused rage to erupt in Vicq's heart. Images of the vampire who'd made him flooded back to Vicq. Zaket had once been Master of the Dresdan Court until he gave up hope of leading a unified Court, and Russo, his most loved Superior, had betrayed him. Vicq's Maker was dead because of Russo. One day he'd avenge his Maker's untimely demise.

Vicq struck, severing the Soldier's head. It landed some ten feet away with the littered parts of the others. He'd probably done the Soldier a favor. The penalty for failing to execute an order was death. Dozens of Russo's Soldiers had failed tonight.

Vicq looked out at his coven members and loyal followers. "Good work. Let's regroup and get back to sanctuary."

CHAPTER SEVEN

❖

Vicq revved the motor of the Ashton Martin and made it through a yellow light only a millisecond before the signal turned red. This particular city district was known for its high crime rate, so he had to watch out for swarming cops and FBI agents. He didn't need to attract attention at the moment. Especially since he was hot on the trail of a black van belonging to the agency he had come to hate so much. No insignia marked the van to identify any affiliation. A normal corporation would have something like that on a company car to market themselves to the public—but not this corporation. Instead, Vicq was able to confirm that the van belonged to the vampire slaughterers by the distinct license plate numbers on the front and back of the vehicle. The plates always began with the letter D, followed by the number 5, and then a series of other distinct numbers and letters. Any time he had ever come in contact with a vehicle belonging to this network, the coding was all the same.

Vicq had just left an antique shop after checking out the new arrivals. He'd found the place by doing a search online seeking more vintage wooden models for his collection. It was only coincidence that he was forced to take a detour that brought him near an orphanage for teen boys where he first spotted the van parked. As he was driving by, the occupants of the van had just concluded their business. The driver had rolled the van door shut before Vicq could get a good look inside. He found their actions strange and highly suspicious. Of course, everything about that organization was suspicious and deceitful.

 Vicq followed the van for another twenty minutes, not sure where it would lead. Finally it turned into the parking lot of *North Heights Health Clinic*. To avoid blowing his cover, he drove by the clinic without stopping. He circled the area, parked the vehicle, and used his abilities to shift through the atmosphere.

 The clinic parking area was empty, except for a

couple stray vehicles near the front and the van he'd followed there, which had been strategically parked near the back. The clinic's operating hours were displayed on the door indicating that it was closed. Most of the lights were turned off inside.

Vicq blended with the shadows and crept to the backside of the building where the van remained idle. The driver had already exited, yet another male sat waiting on the passenger side. A sturdier man wearing blue nursing scrubs came outside from the back door of the clinic to meet the driver. He carried some type of medal box in his hand. Vicq also noticed that the driver had a suitcase. There was a handshake between the men and then a few words were exchanged.

Vicq honed in, calling on his abilities again to pick up on the conversation despite the distance.

"...the heart." The man in the nursing scrubs had just finished talking.

"Here's half of the cash as requested and another delivery." He flipped the suitcase open momentarily to reveal stacks of money. "Three adolescent boys. One with the same blood type as the previous one. If you get us more organs, we'll double the payout."

"I'll need more than double," the man in the scrubs replied.

"You need to call the Heads about that. You want 'em or not? They ain't dead yet, just like you requested." The driver gestured to the rear of the van. "They've all been drugged and are unconscious. That makes it easy for you, right?"

Vicq's blood boiled below the surface and his fangs thrust downward as he realized what was about to transpire. Just earlier, he'd watched the van leave an orphanage and end up at a clinic. Now the men were talking about hearts, adolescent boys, and death. This didn't fair well with Vicq.

The man in scrubs handed the driver the metal box. "Give me my money....and the boys. I've got more bidders lined up. You tell 'em to triple my payout or I'll take another deal."

They made the physical exchange and then the driver produced a set of keys from his pocket and

Prelude

opened the back of the van. Sure enough, there were three boys lying motionless on the floor of the van. The boys had to be no more than thirteen or fourteen years old. Pubescent young boys. Human. Innocent. And they were about to be taken advantage of, and possibly have their organs harvested and sold to the highest bidder.

The men had already begun to drag the boy's bodies from the vans.

Vicq cringed as he processed the situation and acted without another thought. He pulled out a *Kalis* dagger from the sheath in his trench coat and shifted from the man in scrubs to the driver at the foot of the door. He slit their throats one by one. The execution was so sift that the only noise Vicq registered was two limp bodies hitting the pavement and gurgling sounds as they suffocated to death.

The passenger in the van was oblivious to what had just happened, or maybe he really wasn't interested in doing his job anyway. His eyes bulged outward in surprise when Vicq grabbed the van handle and tore the door off the frame. The man shook in fear as his gaze shifted up and down over Vicq. A rubber strip was wrapped around his meaty arm, and he held a syringe filled with clear blue liquid in another. He'd been in there shooting up on those drugs while his partner transacted business. His eyes were glossed over and he seemed high as a kite. It was all the confirmation Vicq needed to conclude that whatever drugs were given to this agency's employers, that it was a harmfully addictive.

Vicq captured him by the shoulders, lifted him up out of the van, and buried his fangs into the man's neck. This wasn't a feeding. He despised taking blood from this scumbag, but he needed to know.

These men worked for that shady organization like scouts. They were killers. They hunted down humans, handed them over to clinics funded by their organization, and brought the organs back to be used in some kind of research lab.

Vicq hadn't realized he had snapped the man's neck until his blood flow began to dwindle, resulting

Prelude

in him having to make more of an effort to take memories. Content on the information he pulled from the criminal, he dropped him carelessly on the ground, and then circled back around to the side of the van where the boys were left. He checked their pulses. They were still alive. Drugged, but still breathing.

At the back of the clinic, Vicq located the gas line and ripped it in two. It didn't take him long to find a lighter in the glove compartment of the van. He torched the clinic. Usually he would watch as it burned to the ground, but not tonight. He picked up the suitcase and moved the boys from the van to the back seat of his Ashton Martin. Because of the small interior, they were nearly piled one on top of the other. They were so drugged up that none of them seemed to care.

This had gone too far. To what lengths would this vampire slaughtering agency go to achieve their self-serving agendas? Kill their own people? Why? For what? Wasn't their mission to ensure continuity? Human continuity?

Vicq drove almost thirty miles until he realized

that the sun would rise soon. He contemplated letting them wake up to see him and to tell them what had happened, but he couldn't keep the boys anyway. They were too young, but at least they were out of harm's way. The orphanage had failed them. Just like his orphanage had failed him when he was just twelve years old. They'd kicked him out on the streets and said he could easily pass for sixteen and get a job. In a way, they were right. Laborers were needed everywhere in Mexico at the time, and most companies didn't care about one's age. At the time, Vicq had no choice and he labored for many years until his fate was turned around.

He spotted a church temple up ahead and steered the car up near the steps. There was one other car parked out front. An old Buick classic with a pink sticker on the back bumper that said: Jesus Saves.

It was almost dawn. He needed to hurry.

Vicq gathered the three young boys and the suitcase in his arms, walked up to the oak double doors, and knocked.

Prelude

An old woman with stark white hair opened one of the doors. She wore a frilly pink and yellow dress and her lips were painted red. Her eyes widened as she glanced upward. Vicq could literally smell the fear rolling off her. The vein near her temple pulsed profusely. Her fingers shook on the doorknob.

Vicq had tried to look human, but he guess it didn't work.

She gasped. "Oh..."

Smoke began to seep from Vicq's skin. The sun was on the rise, burning straight through his flesh. He had to go. He could bolt with the boys still in his arms, but that wouldn't do them any good.

"A-are you the devil?" she asked.

"No."

"Are you here to kill me?"

"No."

"You have children..." she whispered, her eyes sweeping across the load of boys in his arms. She looked surprised and flustered.

"Is this were humans come for help and to be

saved?" Vicq asked.

"Y-y-yes," the old lady stuttered.

He crossed the threshold into the church and the woman stumbled aside, clutching at her heart. He placed the boys on one of the benches.

"These boys are homeless. Will you take care of them?" he asked.

The old lady nodded.

Vicq handed the suitcase the lady. She jumped back, but then took about a minute or two to realize that he meant no harm.

She took the suitcase from him. "Are you coming back for them?"

"Si.... a su debido tiempo," he replied. *In due time.*

Vicq folded away to pursue darkness.

CHAPTER EIGHT

❖

A few days after Elaina and her crew executed the Haegert campus vampires, they were called to a meeting with one of the District heads and his direct report. They sat in a large conference room on one of headquarters' middle levels. The sunshine passing through the large oversized windows filtered across the metal table, providing the only source of light as DH-3 and his direct report shuffled through some papers. Some of the blinds were closed, so half of the room was darker than the other.

Elaina, D-209, D-0008, and D-57 were seated at one end of the table, handed manila folders that were stamped in red with the words highly-classified, and told to hold tight while they finalized some orders.

DH-3 had a laptop on the table and was furiously typing away on the keyboard. Except for the distant squealing noise of the HVAC system, everything was silent. Before DH-3 even began to speak, Elaina knew that her team was here for something big. Perhaps it was the lucrative assignment that Elaina had been waiting for. An assignment that would earn her the recognition she wanted and deserved.

"We've got a Risk Level 10 assignment for your unit. You've been selected based on the diversity of your skillsets. Your training in hand-to-hand combat, direct assault, search and rescue, and sniper missions will help you succeed in this mission. This is not a simple twenty-four-hour assignment. Level 10 assignments can take weeks, even months to complete because of the complexity of the case and the age of the vampire. These types of assignments are passed from one unit to the next until completion. Two units have already failed the mission, resulting in the loss of their lives in the line of duty."

DH-3 paused, linked his fingers together, and let the information sink in.

"This is not a job for a larger unit. A four-member unit, such as yours, is perfect for this type of mission.

Prelude

We're not seeking to mass execute here. Instead, we're looking to capture one vampire in particular. He often roams alone, and from our past experiences dealing with him, he's wary of large crowds and will often stay away from them. We came close last time with only a three-member team. One misstep from one of the trackers resulted in us blowing our cover. This particular vampire knows that we're after him."

DH-3 paused again. "Any questions thus far?"

D-209 shuffled in his chair. "And you want us to execute him?"

DH-3 nodded. "Capture, then execute. We'll need you to drain as much of his blood as you can after the kill. In a previous botched mission, we were only able to salvage a fraction of his blood. He's not a rogue. He's full-blooded Dresdan, and he is powerful. If we can get at least three bags of his blood for research, the scientists believe they can move forward in testing their current theories. He's proven to be too powerful to contain like some of the others we have here, but we want his blood and what we can salvage of his body."

"How do you know he's full-blooded and powerful?" D-0008 questioned.

"We caught him in action. Our cameras recorded less than thirty seconds, but from what we observed, he is no ordinary vampire. He has possible connections to one of the biggest vampire covens in the world, possibly what they call a Court, which is the main network and overruling body."

DH-3 gestured toward a projector, and his direct report reached across the table and flipped the switch. On the darker side, the projector displayed a video clip.

The images on the screen were from one of the botched missions. All Elaina made out were flashes of yellow and white as gunfire blazed on the screen. She made out commands from former unit members as they tried to apprehend the vampire. The vampire itself appeared as one black shadow shifting from one place to the next as it attempted to avoid being wounded. The bullets and arrows were poisoned and could weaken any vampire. All that was required was

Prelude

one clean shot to a major organ or artery. In what seemed like a ten seconds, the gunfire receded, until finally, there was silence. And then the vampire looked right at the camera and the visual went black.

"The van and trackers were reduced to ashes by the time a recovery unit discovered them," DH-3 explained.

"Damn," D-0008 whispered.

"Here's a still shot where you can see his face," DH-3 spoke as his direct report manned the controls of the projector.

Elaina swallowed and leaned forward in her chair.

The picture was fuzzy, but she could still make out his features. He was tall and slim in physique, and although she could not determine what he looked like, she noted that he had a prominent jawline and a defined facial structure. His hair was dark, maybe black. And it was long, hanging way past his shoulders.

"It's the only clear image we have of him. This is the Dresdan you will capture and drain. You will be assigned a van with a vault strong enough to hold and kill him. There is a mechanism inside the vault that will puncture and drain him while inside. The problem is getting him into the vault. You'll have to weaken him, and that's something the last units assigned to the case failed to do." He pointed to the highly classified manila folders. "I suggest you study the contents, notes, and observations provided by both myself and the previous trackers. They will provide useful information into what has worked and what has not worked."

Elaina took the folder.

"Other questions?" DH-3 asked them.

No one said anything.

"Do you accept this assignment?"

"I accept this assignment," D-209 said.

"I accept," Elaina chimed in.

All four members of her unit accepted. Declining wasn't an option, and she almost wondered why the District heads always ended with that question. She supposed they were trying to get rid of the weak links early in their contracts, which is something the District heads were known for. Her unit was literally being thrown to the wolves...er...vampires. She didn't know about anyone else in her crew, but she planned to bounce back a victor.

***

Elaina's unit left the conference room to grab lunch before their scheduled afternoon meeting to go over the folders and devise a plan. She'd declined their invitation to sit and eat with them at the local diner. There was a spot by a shaded tree at a nearby park that she liked to sit under while eating her sandwiches. She figured she'd clear her mind by enjoying a few chapters of a crime thriller novel she hadn't gotten around to reading during the series of intense training sessions.

After swinging her tote bag over her shoulder, she exited the conference room. As she was walking down the corridor, she spotted the young lab tech who'd given her the injection the other day. On instinct, she took a hard left turn and approached the lab tech with a million questions racing through her mind.

"Wait!" Elaina called out.

The lab tech spun around, surprised. Recognition set into her facial expression and she backed away slowly, turned, and half-walked, half-ran in the opposite direction.

Elaina couldn't let the lab tech get away without knowing what had happened to the infected girl and she rushed after her into an unfamiliar area of the building.

She finally caught up to the lab tech halfway down the corridor. "I just want to ask you something," she said.

The lab tech clutched her clipboard to her chest. "What?"

"What's wrong? Why do you look so scared? I'm not going to hurt you," Elaina assured her.

"You're a tracker," the lab tech whispered.

Prelude

"And...?" Elaina was a little confused. Actually, she was more than confused. "We both work here. Do you think I'm going to hurt you?"

The lab tech's posture was rigid and she gave Elaina a silent look. "You were chasing me and you've been trained to kill. I thought..." She shook her head. "Well, I don't know what I thought."

Elaina narrowed her gaze. "You helped me the other day with my injection."

She nodded. "D-33. I remember you."

"Then you also remember what happened with the infected girl."

The lab tech turned swiftly.

Elaina caught her by the arm. "What happened to her?"

"Look, you shouldn't be here," The lab tech looked over her shoulder. "They'll punish you."

"Punish?" Elaina felt the bridge of her nose wrinkle.

"You're not authorized—"

"Look," Elaina urged. "Just tell me what happened to the girl the other day...the infected girl from the Level E, Station B1?"

"She died, okay?" The lab tech shrugged her arm out of Elaina's grasp.

"Okay?" Elaina shook her head. "No, it's not okay."

"She was infected."

"How?"

The lab tech paused and then parted her lips slowly. "She wanted to die."

"Why?"

"She wanted to end her contract. I have to g—."

"Why wasn't anything done to help her live?"

"She was labeled a risk to the District and the mission. She asked to be relieved of her duties."

Elaina stiffened her posture. "Asking to be relieved of duties, doesn't sound like a wish to die? So which is it, did she want to die or did she want help?"

"I was told she wanted to die when she came in with the infection."

Prelude

"Which level did she work on?"

"*A*. Look, why are you asking me this?"

"A? Level A is where all the files are kept. *Level A employees rarely ever come in contact with vampires,*" Elaina replied. "Did someone deliberately poison her?"

"I don't know anything." The lab tech shifted her gaze to the floor. "I have to go. I shouldn't be telling you this. I wouldn't repeat this to anyone or something will happen to you too," she warned.

The lab tech turned and dash off down the hall, disappearing through a set of metal double doors. Elaina stood there for a couple minutes, lost in a sea of overlapping thoughts.

CHAPTER NINE

❖

Any assignment involving a stakeout was an assignment Elaina sought the most. Even before she'd joined District 5, she enjoyed people watching. She observed what made people tick and grow angry and what made them overjoyed and happy. People she couldn't read piqued her interests the most. Oftentimes, she found that those were the individuals who had more than the current state of affairs on their minds. Kind of like she did right now…

Had she made the right choice with her life?

Although she felt a sense of pride in knowing that her job kept murderers off the streets, was this really her purpose?

With sixteen years of being homeschooled and directed by her devoted mother behind her, one would think she'd know exactly what she wanted. But that was far from the truth. Not interested in the big-time

Ivy League colleges that had sent her solicitations to apply, she'd attended a local community college instead. Had even changed her major four times in the three years that she'd studied there.

First it had been computer science, since she didn't really want to deal with people on a daily basis, and then it was physics because she'd always been interested in learning how to preserve the Earth's natural resources. Then, one Thanksgiving, she'd talked with her parents over turkey and dressing and they'd mentioned that a prominent university had sent home a flyer about recruiting students for their new Genomics program. They told her how the program had recently added a research and study group on the history of vampires. By that time, most adults knew they existed. There wasn't much the authorities could do to keep their existence a secret since rogues had already begun to prey on and kill humans.

Since her dad was on a first-name and friendly basis with the professor at the university the flyer had come from, getting in was rather easy. Of course, her

Prelude

perfect GPA score at the community college spoke for itself, but sometimes it was whom one knew that counted.

Her professor, Arnold Wade, had strong connections with District 5. He may have even been on the payroll in addition to his employment with the university, but he'd never told Elaina anything about it. Within months, a District recruiter approached Elaina with a lucrative but risky job offer.

Eventually, she'd get to work in the labs and use her Genetics research studies, but first she'd have to work her way up.

She was given a choice: clerical or front line duties.

She'd never liked being anyone's assistant. In fact, she aspired to be a leader. Working her way up from the front line seemed the best path for her.

"Elaina...Elaina, do you see him from your position?"

D-209's voice jolted her back to reality, and she blinked twice and trained her gaze back on the dilapidated warehouse across the street. She crouched lower behind the bushes and scanned the area.

"Fuck…I don't see a thing," she said, cursing herself for drifting off in thought.

"It's him, dammit," D-57 said. "I can see him on my side from inside the van."

They could communicate with each other via mic on a designated channel.

"This is our chance. It's been almost a week. Fuck it. We have to do this," D-209 said. "Are y'all ready?"

Elaina was about to admit her mistake, but that's when she saw the vampire and another suspect near the corner of the building. It was about an hour past midnight, so the area was obscured in darkness except for a few faulty lamps up the road, shedding some light on the scene.

You couldn't make out his companion at all, but there was a fifty percent chance that this was their vamp. They'd tracked a source to this very location where several drug and other criminal busts had gone down.

"Elaina?" D-209 urged. "Got my back?"

D-209 was the first shooter tonight, which meant he would pull the trigger while the others spotted.

She checked the tightness of her clip at her side and reached down to make sure her weapons were still strapped tautly to her boots. "Yeah."

"He's turning...he's turning around..." This came from D-57 in the van.

"I've got a shot," D-209 whispered. "I'm going in—shit!"

After the first shot had rung out, the vampire swung around, startled. A second shot was fired, but it hit the ground near the vampire's boot instead of him. Dust rose up, but the vampire had long since shifted from that spot.

D-209, aka Danny, had lousy aim. She could have done better than that. Now the vampire knew someone was on to him. And she certainly wasn't going to stand there in the shadows and let it kill her. She came out of her hiding place and covered for Danny as she was instructed to do.

"The vamp's assailant got away," D-57 reported from the van. "The fucking roof...vampire suspect on the fucking roof!"

Elaina dodged behind a broken down rusty car in the parking lot, gripping her gun tightly. The air whipped tightly across her face and rushed through her ears, making it hard for her to use her sense of hearing to track the vampire.

Vamps usually made swooshing noises as they fled past their victim, or, in this case, their threat.

"D-0008, come in," D-209 urged. "0008?"

"He's...got...me. Roof..." D-0008 didn't sound so hot as he rasped across the channel.

"Oh, shit," D-209 exclaimed.

Suddenly there was a loud thud. Elaina shot up from behind the van, weapon aimed to fire. The vampire had jumped from the roof onto the ground with D-0008 by the neck. His feet were about three

Prelude

inches off the ground as the vampire held him high but positioned strategically in front of his own body.

"Why are you hunting me?" the vampire asked. Its eyes blazed red. A common trait in the most powerful Dresdan, and the color only came out when they were mad or high on emotions.

"Drop him, vamp!" D-209 ordered.

"That's not how it works. You came for me. This is the problem you created," the Dresdan said. Long black hair floated in the wind, gracefully, yet the creature held D-0008 with inhuman force that turned his face white.

D-209 fired a warning shot near the vampire.

It laughed. "What a fucking waste! You're garbage."

In that instant, the van came plowing across the parking lot, nearly swiping Elaina as it hit top speed. Apparently, it wasn't fast enough for a vampire. The creature shifted out of the way just in time, but D-0008 never made it.

Elaina cringed and diverted her gaze from the

carnage. She took that moment to open fire after the vampire.

"Go, go, go," D-209 urged as they followed the vampire to the dilapidated building.

Elaina led the way, every one of her senses on alert while D-209 followed far behind her. There were no lights inside. The only thing that greeted them was the smell of dirty motor oil, engine grease, and rust.

D-209 fired behind her and only succeeded in busting through a row of paint cans.

"What?" she yelled at him, startled.

"I thought it was him," D-209 said.

"Control yourself. Aim to kill. Don't just shoot in the air aimlessly. You're giving us away," she warned.

"Fuck that. That thing isn't going to kill me."

"Shut the fuck up before you give our location away."

"I can hear you two," the vampire drawled from a location unknown to Elaina. "Amateur assassins. They send you all the time, knowing you will die." The

Prelude

vampire laughed.

"Come out, come out, wherever you are," Elaina taunted.

"I love the way you sing to me, human," the vampire said. "I just might."

His reply made Elaina feel uncomfortable. Not afraid, but uncomfortable. That was odd, given that her life was on the line. Fuck her comfort, she wanted to get out of here alive.

"Do I need to ram the place? Jake's dead, man," D-57 reported, his voice muddled, yet came through as panicked.

"W-we'll h-have to abort," D-209 stuttered.

Elaina couldn't turn to give him the side-eye with her motivation still centered around finding their target, but she said, "No fucking way! We finish this. Come on out, vamp."

In a turn of events that caught Elaina off guard, the vampire came to a screeching halt right in front of them. A bullet blasted Elaina in the leg, and she cried out. She had no idea who'd shot the bullet until D-209 shoved her right at the vampire.

"Take her!"

He dashed out of the warehouse and left her there in the darkness.

The vampire had a stronghold on her arm, and when she raised her gaze to confirm her dilemma, his eyes flashed red.

A scream caught in her throat, and her life literally flashed before her eyes. Fear. She hadn't felt it in a long time. Someone had the upper hand against her, and that had provoked her fear.

"I've come out," the Dresdan said. "Isn't that what you wanted?"

Elaina opened her mouth, but no words left her lips. She heard a motor rev up outside and some tires scraping the dirt. Her heart dropped when she realized what had just transpired. Where her heart seemed absent, anger rose in its place.

Her leg burned like hell where D-209's bullet had

Prelude

grazed her. Good thing the bullet wasn't poisoned. She would have been out like a light...and probably the vampire's snack by now.

"You are too beautiful to be my executioner," the Dresdan drawled. His accent was foreign and exotic. She could tell English wasn't his native language.

Elaina examined him. He looked different up close. Almost like a man. Almost human. He was... striking. Handsome. Yet, lethal and deadly.

The Dresdan turned her so that she was facing away from him and brushed his nose against the bun secured to the back of her head. He then sniffed behind her ear.

"Your blood smells like sunshine. Funny... sunshine is the thing I detest the most, yet it is the thing I most want to conquer."

"I am no sunshine, vampire. Let me go," she finally said.

"You came for me, beautiful." The Dresdan inhaled deeply. "Your blood flows freely like an evening shower. Just an inch more and your colleague would have killed you."

He was referring to the bullet that had grazed her leg.

"If you're going to drink me, you might as well go ahead and kill me first. Don't play cat and mouse with me. I don't play nice," she shot back at him.

He chuckled deeply. "I work for my meals, sunshine. And I don't prey on the weak."

Weak. That word didn't resonate with her. She didn't like being called weak, but she held her tongue. She'd much rather have the vampire believe she was weak and decide she wasn't worth it, than come to the conclusion that she was strong and hunt her down for the kill.

"What will you do to me?" she asked.

"I just want to know who sent you and exactly where I can find them," the Dresdan said.

She felt his fingers trailing down the side of her body. She tried to wriggle from his grip, but he held

Prelude

her to his chest. She expected it to be cold and hard, like an unmoving, undead person, yet surprisingly, he was far from that. Almost human, yet not entirely.

"That's classified," she said.

"Would you rather I drink you?" he asked.

"Won't do you any good. I've been trained to hide memories," she replied.

"Trained, but can you? Don't take me for a rogue. I'm Dresdan, and if I wanted to, I could drain every last memory you have."

She frowned. "Is that a threat?"

His fingers grazed over the wound on her leg. He lifted his hand, coming up with blood, and then his arm disappeared behind her.

It didn't take Elaina long to realize that he'd tasted her.

The Dresdan inhaled sharply and then stiffened. "Sunshine...but you are irresistible, despite the drugs in your system."

"I don't do drugs."

"You shot up with the same drugs as the last weak group of trackers they sent after me," he said.

Elaina bit her tongue. She shouldn't have to explain to this Dresdan that the drugs she'd shot up with were to prevent infection should she come in contact with any of his blood.

Elaina would have never imagined she would be this fucking close to a vampire.

"So, am I going to have to drink you to get what I want?" he asked.

"Looks that way." She shrugged. "But like I said, I don't play nice, so you'd better kill me first."

"I don't drink from dead humans, either," he said.

"Then it looks like you won't eat tonight," she said.

"We'll see." He breathed against her neck.

Elaina acted quickly. Grabbing the dagger from her belt loop, she spun around, slashed the sharp end against the Dresdan's chest, and pulled out a handgun.

She fired near his head, missing by only a fraction. A few strands of his glossy black hair fell onto his right

Prelude

shoulder.

The Dresdan never even flinched. In fact, he stood there, unmoving with those deadly red eyes of his and fangs so thick and long that Elaina almost passed out from the sight of them.

"You're not afraid of dying, are you?" she asked, gun held tightly in her hand.

He laughed. The cut she'd made on his chest with the knife began to heal. "Why would you ask a vampire that question?"

"I'd ask anyone that question."

"Are you insinuating that I am just anyone?"

Elaina's eyes flickered over him again. Head to toe and back again. Almost human. Only more. Her gaze shot back to his and she tightened her fist around the butt of the gun.

"No, I'm not," she said, aiming for his chest.

He shook his head. "A bullet in the chest won't kill me."

"The bullet won't..." She narrowed her gaze,

challenging him.

"If you shoot me with that thing, you want to make sure it kills me." He grinned. "Do you have a clear shot?" He pushed off the wall.

"Take another step, bastard, and I'll blow your brains out."

He cocked an eyebrow at her. "Sounds like you mean it."

"I do."

"Your colleague betrayed you. You need to be saving those bullets for him."

Fury rose in her chest. Yes, she would kill that rat bastard.

"You're hesitating because you don't want to kill me," he said, lowering his voice a little.

She swallowed.

"I know why you don't..."

She pressed her lips together but didn't respond.

"You've been told lies about me and my kind and you know it. We're not the murderers you were taught

Prelude

to believe."

"Liar!"

"Who are you going to trust?"

"Not you!"

"No, not me. But whom? A vampire-killing, mafia organization that sends you out here after me to certain death...or your instincts?"

"Lies," she whispered.

"They sent you here to die. You're a pawn. How much of my blood are they trying to steal? How much more do they want? Do they even know what they are doing?" He pondered, his tone of voice growing in irritation by the second. "What are the lives of four trackers worth to gain a pint of Dresdan blood when they have hundreds more sheep ready take commands without question and are recruiting by the dozens?"

Her temperature rose and her lips parted in shock.

"Oh? You didn't know. There are lots of things you don't know...Elaina."

"How do you know my name?"

"Lots of memories reside in the blood. It only takes a drop." His eyes changed from deep red to black, and his gaze fell to her thigh where blood seeped against her leather and drained down her leg.

The injury wouldn't kill her, but if she didn't get treatment for it soon, there was a chance it could become infected.

"Tell me, sunshine, are *you* afraid of dying?" he asked.

"No," she stated without hesitation.

"Then what would you die for? An organization that doesn't give a rat's ass about your life, or a cause that benefits more than just a few greedy shareholders?"

The warehouse was silent as she pondered his questions, but it was too late, he'd already raised the doubts within her.

"Ah, you have reservations about all of this."

The Dresdan extended his hand toward her. She jumped back right before she realized there were keys in his palm.

Prelude

"What is that?"

"My offer. I'll give you three days to think about it, and then I want you to answer me."

She shook her head. "Who do you think I am? Your child?"

"I don't know who you are. You seem to be confused about who and what you represent." He shrugged. "The choice is yours. Freedom and a set of wheels to get you out of the ghetto where your organization sent you to be slaughtered."

Elaina frowned. "I can walk."

"Si?" He tossed her a skeptical look.

She held out her hand, and he dropped the keys in her palm.

"What's your n—?"

Before she could get the last word out, he was gone, leaving her standing in the middle of the abandoned, old, dilapidated building.

This place could have been her resting place. She could have died. But by luck, she was still here.

Once outside, it didn't take long for Elaina to find the car the vampire had offered her. She sped off into the night, but she wasn't headed to her condo. She was probably believed to be dead, and until her mind was made up, she'd pretend to be for the time being.

CHAPTER TEN

❖

Four nights had passed when Elaina finally decided to ditch the hotel she'd been lying low at to call a District head. The vampire hadn't shown his face as promised, but Elaina had already made up her mind by then.

She'd signed a contract with District 5. There was no getting out of it.

The phone rang twice before someone picked up. "This is DH-3."

"This is D-33, checking in."

"We have you on the records as deceased," he said, his tone uncaring. "You and D-0008."

"I was severely injured and abandoned by my unit with no phone access. I only just recovered enough to report in. I couldn't move for days," she said, half telling the truth.

"Do you need me to send medical assistance?"

"No. I've managed thus far." Her mom had been

a paramedic before she quit to take care of Elaina when she was first born, so Elaina knew how to reduce the symptoms of almost any ailment and dress many wounds.

"There were plans to replace the two of you," DH-3 said. "The assignment has been shifted to another unit until further notice, but these are serious allegations against your fellow unit members. It's against protocol to leave a dying colleague behind, especially after being attacked by vampires."

"They were only doing their jobs," she said, carefully. "I was...held against my will by a vampire. I fought him off. Killed him."

"Good work on killing a mere rogue, but D-209 reported that our main target has yet to be located."

So D-209 had lied. About everything. It meant he didn't want the District heads aware that he'd had the main vampire suspect contained in a building but had instead pushed her and ran like a cowering bitch.

Elaina contained her anger. "He hasn't been captured," she confirmed.

Prelude

"It's quitting time, D-33. Report first thing in the morning for further instructions. You and what's left of your unit. Understood?" DH-3 ordered.

When Elaina hung up with him, she triple checked to make sure that all of her doors and windows were locked and her curtains were pulled taught. Her unit members didn't even know she was alive. When she saw D-209 again, she wasn't sure that she would be able to contain her anger enough to keep from lashing out. She wanted to kill him. If he betrayed her once, he'd betray her again.

CHAPTER ELEVEN

❖

Elaina woke up to tapping noises on the sliding glass doors of her balcony. She grumbled, seriously hoping that whatever bird or night owl had landed on her terrace would go away. She'd tossed and turned the previous nights after lying on a hard mattress waiting for her leg to heal. Now she was finally back in her own bed, and if she wanted to confront D-209 tomorrow and convince a District head to put her in another unit, she'd need all the rest she could get.

But the tapping did not stop.

She picked up a fluffy pillow and pulled it over her head. Then she heard the Dresdan's call.

"Elaina."

What the fuck?

She jolted up in bed and her attention immediately flew to the balcony doors. The curtains were pulled and she couldn't see a thing. Half unbelieving and half mortified, she tiptoed over to the door and peeled back the vertical blinds.

Sure enough, a dark figure stood on her balcony, silky, black hair flowing in the breeze. When she gasped, he turned around and grinned at her.

Elaina backed away about two feet, shaking her head. The blinds fell back in place, and the image of the Dresdan disappeared.

"No, no. I'm not seeing this," she told herself. She peeled the blinds back again and he was still there. "Fuck."

Had he come to kill her? Finish what he started? Four nights had already passed. He hadn't kept his end of the bargain.

The vampire held up his hands, palms facing her, and then he made a peace sign.

Elaina turned around and looked toward the foyer of her condo. What was wrong with her? Why was she paranoid? No one would burst in here unannounced. She had no friends. Didn't get any visitors. It was well

Prelude

past midnight, and the whole building was probably asleep except for a handful of night staff.

She unlocked the balcony door, slid it open, and a gush of fresh air flooded inside. Her heart picked up tempo when she realized there was nothing between her and the Dresdan.

"My name is Vicq," the Dresdan said.

"Vicq," she repeated. "Just Vicq?"

"When I was made, I gave up my last name."

It was difficult to remember that he was a vampire. He was so calm and civilized. D5 had taught all recruits and trackers that vampires were vicious, wild creatures. Vicq was not vicious or wild.

"Are you going to invite me inside?"

"Depends."

"On what?"

"Are you going to kill me?"

He took a moment to answer her as his Adam's apple bobbed slowly on his throat. "No."

"Come in, but remember...I don't play nice."

"Duly noted," he said and crossed the threshold. His gaze roamed over her area and he moved around, observing her things.

She slid the door closed again, applied the locks, and pulled the curtains shut.

"How did you find me?"

"Your blood," he answered.

"Is it that simple?"

"No. But when a Dresdan becomes addicted to a human after just one little taste, he'll trace the source anywhere...even to Hell."

Elaina chuckled. "You can't be addicted to me."

He closed in then, and she stumbled back until she landed butt first on the bed. Her heart beat frantically as he knelt slightly, taking her leg and cradling it in his hand.

He slid his fingers under her long nightgown and brushed the fabric away to reveal her thigh. The wound where the bullet had grazed her was still fresh.

Elaina should have pulled away, but she didn't. He

Prelude

bent low and pressed his lips to her thigh. Her loins tightened and her center pulsed. His tongue was hot against her wound as he stroked the healing skin. He let her leg fall and then rose again.

"What the..." She looked down at her leg, only to discover that she was now completely healed. The skin was like new. Not even a nurse would realize that a bullet had grazed her there. "How did you do that?"

"My saliva carries healing properties. You should know that. Your organization keeps records of these things. Yet, only a select few of you are made aware. I wonder why that is..." He winked at her.

"You healed me." She rubbed at her leg. "This is insane and unreal."

"Have you made up your mind?"

"I have," she said.

"And?"

"I'm here for the long haul. I kill rogue vampires for a living. I have no problem with that." She shrugged.

"You don't have to stand by a faulty mission to kill

rogues for a living."

"You think our mission is faulty only because I kill creatures like you," she said, standing and walking in a circle around him. His trench coat prevented a complete inspection, but considering this was her second time being so close to a vampire, her view would have to do for now.

"I don't think. I *know*. Your organization kills unjustly. I have evidence."

"Why are you here, Vicq? If it's to ridicule my employer, you should leave," she said, motioning toward the door.

"Why did you let me in? If it's because you don't completely trust your employer to tell you the real truth, why don't you just admit it?"

She swallowed. "Why do they want your blood so badly?"

"I was made by a Master vampire. He was nearly one thousand years old, almost impossible to kill until someone he trusted betrayed him."

Prelude

He ventured farther into her one-bedroom condo, walked over to her closet, pressed the collar of a shirt to his nose, and inhaled deeply.

"What did you do to become a District target?" She figured if he were supplying answers, she'd continue inquiring.

"I find anything and anyone linked to them—especially where the funding comes from—and I destroy it. I have burned banks to the ground and rummaged through vaults belonging to D5. And once I find a way to infiltrate their headquarters, I'll destroy that too."

"Why do you do it?"

"They've killed and captured dozens of us. Probably more than that. We're beaten, studied, mutilated, and treated like savages. We're not all rogues. Your organization just doesn't understand the fundamentals of our society. We were executing rogues who carried out acts of violence just fine before this organization came into existence and labeled all of us murderers."

"But if you were handling your rogue population, they wouldn't be a problem right now."

"Truth. But is it not true that your organization is more concerned with creating some kind of hybrid human mutant than they are about helping your government control the rogue population?" he countered.

"There are many missions," she said. "Each division carries out a different mission. Mine is to keep deadly rogue vampires from preying on humans."

"What about the mission that involves studying humans against their will. Picking up humans off the street and deliberately trying to infect them with bad blood in an effort to proceed with the organization's experimentation."

Elaina cringed as a memory of the infected young girl in the labs came back to her. She had never found out how the girl became infected.

"And you have evidence of all of this?"

"I have my sources within your network," he said

Prelude

and then dismissed the issue. "By the way, I killed your partner."

"Excuse me?"

"Just before landing here outside your room, I found out where he slept. They'll find him one day, floating in the lake miles away from here. There's no use going to look for him. He'll enjoy it there for now. He seems to like water from what I took from his memory. It's where his wife was found just last year."

"Do you mean Danny?"

"Danny, yeah, that was his name. His blood was tainted. He committed a lot of felony crimes in his days before joining that vampire slaughtering agency. He seemed worried about the case revolving around the disappearance of his new wife. Something about an insurance policy and a hitman. The images were fuzzy. He did a good job using his training to try and hide them but like I said, I'm no dirty rogue. He thought you were dead, you know? He was actually glad he had killed you. After drinking him, I was going to let him live, but then he had such nasty, non-remorseful thoughts about what he'd done to you that I couldn't help but to drain him lifeless."

Bile rose in Elaina's throat. "You had no right."

"You were going to seek revenge, weren't you, Elaina?" Vicq grinned.

"I was. The day would have come, and I would have acted then. I didn't need your help."

"You don't belong with these low-life convicts. Are you ready to answer my question?" he asked. "Will you die for this dirty, ratty organization of yours, or do you want your freedom again?"

"Again?"

"I visited you on the fourth night as you made the call and voiced your decision. You could have walked free, Elaina, but instead, you walked back into a trap. They are using you, and they will use you until there is nothing else left of you but a bag of blood on a shelf or a vat of ashes."

A nerve literally popped in Elaina's throat. "Get out!" She pointed to the door.

Prelude

"Very well," Vicq said. "Should we give it another three days?"

Elaina stormed over to the balcony doors, threw it open, and pointed into the night. "Don't come back. I could be severely reprimanded for inviting a vampire here."

"Ah, but you didn't invite me. I came to you. It is not every day that a vampire can venture near sunlight, but you are sunshine to me. The only sunshine I will ever come to."

Vicq turned and folded away into the night. Elaina's leg tingled where he had kissed it. That night, Elaina realized that she would be forever connected to this Dresdan.

CHAPTER TWELVE

Elaina came to understand that being without a work unit was no fun. No one wanted to work together where there was no uniformity. For over a week, she'd been organizing deliveries between District headquarters and a government storage facility where they kept an overflow of weapons.

Following the disbanding of her crew, she'd been moved to a clerical post until she was reassigned to a unit or another one was created.

Elaina walked down the row of boxes, double-checking the serial numbers against the data on her clipboard. She grumbled as she moved. This was not her idea of actual work; it was just busy work. The only thing that had come from the change was that she was the lead on the project—one step closer to her goals.

"D-33?" One of the guys peeked his head into the storage unit. "We're all set. Should I send the next truckload back to headquarters?"

"Yes, do that. Also, select someone to stay behind and help lock up. It's time to close up shop and head out. It's getting late, and I want to get an early start tomorrow morning."

He nodded. "Sure thing."

If everyone at District 5 were as nice and sensible as that young man, she'd probably find that being in the same room or space with them for several hours a day wasn't so bad after all.

Elaina grabbed her duffle bag and checked it to make sure that her keys were inside. She wasn't in the mood to go through all of the security checks for gaining entry when someone lost their set of keys. Security was so tight that most things were on lockdown or required three levels of approvals these days. Plus, most of the staff had already clocked out that evening. Now, every time she left this place, she made sure that her keys were with her.

Something exploded outside, but it took Elaina more than a second to realize that the sounds that

Prelude

followed were the panicked screams of her colleagues. She rushed out of the storage building and saw a fireball near the left gate where an eighteen-wheeler had either been bombed or set on fire.

The sun had barely receded, yet a handful of vampires had made haste in attacking them. Two workers were already dead.

Elaina dropped her duffle bag to the ground, grabbed her Glock from the holster on her hip, and opened fire at the throng of swarming vampires. She couldn't tell if they were weaker rogues or Dresdan. They worked in a team, debilitating the few workers that hadn't left for the day.

What a coincidence that they had enough weapons here to start a small war, but most were locked up in boxes waiting to be shipped to headquarters. Not to mention, the vamps had bombed a truckload of that supply. Despite the immediate availability of weaponry around them, these District 5 workers weren't trained to fight. A few were probably trackers or had been—like herself. But many here had been re-assigned to this station until their official post was provided to them. Stocking weaponry wasn't Elaina's idea of a frontline duty assignment. This wasn't exactly the average clerical work either. In either case, the attack had caught everyone off guard, including Elaina.

As she fired a series of rounds at her targets, a vampire blocked her path. She sheathed her Glock quickly and pulled out a set of daggers. There was no use trying to shoot at close range. When a vampire stood within a few feet of its target, the best way to fend for oneself was the use of hand-to-hand combat force or small weaponry like her daggers.

The vampire was quick, but she used her training to anticipate his moves. Luckily, he still moved around and fought like a human, which told her that this one was, in fact, a young rogue.

Her break came when his back was turned. She propelled herself forward and drove her dagger straight down into his spine. The vampire flung itself forward, turned, and ran straight for her. Pushing off the ground with the balls of her feet, she leapt about

Prelude

two feet in the air and executed a jumping axe kick. The vampire took the blow to the upper chest and landed on the ground in front of her. When he regained his balance, she hook-kicked him across the side of the face. She dropped her daggers while the vampire was still down trying to pop his spine back into place, grabbed her Glock, and shot the creature twice in the head.

As she moved forward to finish off more vamps, she reloaded her Glock.

The scene before her wasn't pretty. Several of her colleagues were lying dead on the ground. She picked up another weapon from the ground, raced up behind an unsuspecting vampire from behind while he was feeding on one of the dead, and sliced through the middle of his neck with a machete she found lying nearby on the ground.

When Elaina looked up again from the carnage, that's when she saw him. Vicq. A dark figure approaching the scene as if he owned the place. At first, she could have believed that he was responsible for the wreckage, but then he began to murder his own kind. He grabbed them, one by one, and snapped their necks for an easy execution. All the while, her colleagues labeled him a threat just like the others and continued to pump him full of bullets. Blood wept from his wounds as he expelled the bullets. That's when Elaina realized that what was left of her crew was no match for a Dresdan.

They couldn't kill Vicq. He was unstoppable. It was why D5 wanted his blood and why they wanted him dead.

Odd though. Elaina didn't want him dead. From the moment she had exchanged words with him in that old dilapidated warehouse, to the days that had gone by without him returning to her condo, she'd been harboring the very same intuition that rose in her gut now. An intuition that went against everything District 5 had ever taught her—Vicq wasn't the enemy.

All the rogues had fallen, most of them by Vicq's hand. The only people who remained standing were herself, two of her colleagues, and Vicq.

Prelude

As Vicq closed the gap between Elaina and himself, her colleagues continued to shoot, clueless to what she already knew. Vicq was trying to protect her.

Blood leaked from his mouth and down against his fangs as his pace slowed.

They were killing him. Elaina let go of her weapons and dashed toward him.

"Stop!" she yelled. "Stop shooting."

Of course, they wouldn't listen. A District 5's employee's number one rule was to kill all vampires on sight.

When her body collided with Vicq's, she linked his arm around her and rushed him toward the metal storage unit. A bullet caught her in the shoulder as she ran. She cried out once, but kept pushing toward safety. Once they were inside and she had bolted the doors, only then did the shooting stop.

Vicq slumped to the floor, sitting up against the wall. "Elaina, are you okay?"

"Yes." She choked on her words as the pain from

the bullet in her shoulder began to consume her.

"I'm sorry I didn't get here sooner."

She knelt beside him. "What? You knew about this?"

"No...I've been watching you."

She shook her head. "I don't understand."

He lifted his hand and stroked her cheek. His hands were surprisingly soft, and she exhaled softly, trying to focus on how good his touch felt instead of the bullet inside her.

"I'll protect you now," he said. "I don't trust your mafia organization with your life."

"You have to understand. You have to stay away from me and from anything connected to the District. They're going to kill you if you don't stay away from me." She reached behind her and tested the severity of the open wound with her fingers. She cringed. "Fuck..."

"You're hurt. Let me heal you," he said.

"Vicq..."

He held his hand out, palm side up. "Trust me.

Prelude

Come closer."

Elaina crept close, knelt between his thighs, and bowed her head. She grimaced as he peeled the leather aside and ripped it away from the bullet hole. When he dug the slug out, she screamed. Relief finally came when he pressed his lips to her wound. She felt the sting of his healing powers as the serum in his saliva coursed through her flesh.

"Elaina, I have to...slumber. It's imminent, but I'd rather will it myself. I've lost too much blood, but I'm not leaving you out here to go back to them."

"Slumber?"

"It's how a Dresdan heals, but slumber must happen in a safe place. Not here."

"I can't go with you."

"Then I won't go."

"You have to. Please," she urged. "My crew is still out there. Soon they will call to report this mess. They saw me bring you in here. They will kill you."

"This is precisely why you must come with me. I

can't risk losing you because of how you helped me." She swallowed.

This time he opened both of his arms, inviting her to embrace him. "I have just enough strength to shift one hundred miles. It will be quick. All you'll feel is rapid movement."

"Where will you take me?" she asked.

"Someplace where you'll be safe. A house near the countryside."

Elaina hesitated, but then she heard the footsteps of her colleagues just outside the storage warehouse. They weren't going to relent until Vicq was dead, and she had no idea how she would explain herself. She'd assisted a vampire. The same vampire that she'd been assigned to execute. Time after time, she'd failed her mission. She had failed it on purpose.

She glanced at Vicq again. His eyes weren't red anymore, but rather a dull hazel. Almost human, but not entirely. He was weak. Vulnerable.

"*Ven conmigo*," he whispered. "Come with me."

CHAPTER THIRTEEN

❖

Elaina couldn't sleep.

Not because there was a vampire slumbering in the lowest level of the countryside manor. Not because the home had very few windows and steel doors. She was fatigued, and her eyes were heavy, but she had this inclination to observe everything around her.

She hadn't gone outside yet since it was still dark, but when she looked out the window she spotted nothing but fields of straw and hay under the moonlight. She would have never imagined that she would be here, taking refuge in a vampire's home. With a vampire slumbering only one story below her in an underground vault.

Vicq's injury must have been severe because the moment they'd touched down in the foyer, he'd told her that the home was stocked with everything she'd need and then disappeared. Moments later, she'd heard footsteps on the level below her and a loud thud as if someone had closed a door. She'd understood what he had done, and her uneasiness had soon worn off as she ventured from room to room, admiring the intricate wall paintings; old, refurbished English style furnishings, and wood carvings.

The miniature carvings were what fascinated her the most. They were on almost every flat surface of the home. There were wooden cranes and other animals. Carvings and depictions of people and buildings. Bowls, utensils, pedestals. As far as Elaina could see, there were hundreds of them.

Elaina wondered if he'd made them? What had his life been like in the past? What did he think of his life now?

And what would her life become now that she'd committed a District offense by befriending a vampire—and not just any vampire—a Dresdan.

A carved, wooden owl sat on the mantle of the brick fireplace. She traced the perfectly cut ridges with

Prelude

the pads of her fingers...

***

Vicq would have followed the scent of Elaina's blood anywhere, so finding her looking at some pieces on his mantle was easy. He'd gained enough of his strength back by shutting his body down for a few hours. Now he hungered for the very thing that would empower him the most. But first, he had to see the woman that intrigued him. The female that stirred something so deeply within him that he hadn't really figured out what it was yet. It had been so long since he'd felt the need to protect anyone like he did Elaina. He would protect his coven members, yes. But with Elaina, his urge to safeguard her was different.

He stood in the doorway for a few minutes, observing the fluidity of her motions as she walked through his great room. Her hair was deep brown, long, and naturally curly. She could have almost been a hair model or a beauty queen, yet she'd chosen a profession not normally entered by women of her caliber. Her skin was a golden honey color and soft to the touch. She was taller than most women, but not as tall as him. The leather boots she always wore brought the top of her head to his chin. He remembered how her hair had smelled like sunshine when she was thrown into his arms that very first night.

Her cheekbones were high and her lips were full. She barely ever smiled, but Vicq wanted to change that. Somehow, he'd have to convince her to stay with him...and he would make her happy. Whatever he had to do to make her happy, he would do it.

She raised her hand to rub the back of her neck, and that's when Vicq saw the 5 mark that he'd come to recognize and hate. Those scumbags she worked for had burned their brand right into her flesh. She was marked as an enemy to his kind.

But his enemy was also the woman he wanted for himself. But not just for her blood...

In that moment, Elaina turned to look at him and

Prelude

gasped.

"How long have you been standing there?"

"I lost track of time admiring your beauty," he replied.

Her large brown eyes sparkled, and she pressed her lips together and narrowed her gaze. "You love people watching? Is that why you've been spying on me?"

"I just love watching you."

"So..." She circled him, her eyes sweeping up and down the length of him. "Are you all better now?"

"Not entirely. I want to feed."

She stopped walking around him, and he picked up on a tinge of fear.

"Don't worry, I know how to contain myself."

"You're not thinking about biting me, are you?" she asked.

"Why would you ask a vampire that question?"

"Is that why you brought me here?"

"I wouldn't have brought you here just to bite

you," he said. "My other reasons are more important."

"And they are?"

"Protection being one. Courtship being the other."

She arched a perfect brow. "Courtship?"

He moved to the sofa where she stood and held out his arm, welcoming her to take a seat. "Or friendship," he said. "Sometimes you'll have to question me about these things. I wasn't born in your time, and English isn't my first language. My father spoke Pangasinan and my mother spoke Spanish. They used them interchangeably, depending on their moods. I spoke very little English before I was made, which I learned through the blood of others."

She took a seat. "Have you ever courted anyone before?"

"No. It's not often that I find someone whose blood satisfies all my needs and even awakens some others."

"You're very frank," she said, giving him a warning glance.

"I don't know how not to be."

Prelude

"Well, in case you haven't noticed, I've never befriended a vampire, or courted one. That word sounds so strange. Where are you from?"

He took a seat close beside her on the sofa. "I grew up in the Philippines where my parents lived together for a short time. My mother's family was from Mexico and they were merchants. When she was sixteen, she met my father after her family sailed to Luzon to trade. My father courted my mother during the months her family remained. She became pregnant with me, and her family left her behind. I was born out of wedlock. My parents made their living as woodworkers in the Philippines, and then again for a short time in Mexico."

"Woodworkers?" She glanced around the room. "Did they make the pieces throughout your home?"

"No, they're something I collect to remind me of them. My parents were killed in an earthquake in Mexico when I was nine. The owl on the mantle was made by my mother, however."

"I'm sorry about your parents. When were you made into a vampire?" she asked.

"About sixty-three years ago. I was twenty-nine at the time," he said. "I had spent the previous twenty years of my human life working as a farmer, sometimes migrating into the US to work. It wasn't an easy time back then. I wasn't suicidal, but I often wondered what my purpose was. I met Zaket almost by chance. He noticed me, and watched me working in the fields for several years before approaching me. Zaket was unique in his way of thinking and in his reasoning. He's never made anyone a vampire as a result of their imminent death. Every vampire he's ever made was healthy with no signs of death on the horizon. From our first meeting, he revealed to me what he was and how he lived. *Vampiro*, I called him, but little did I know then that many vampire breeds existed. I was fascinated by his vision and I wanted what he had. I chose death to rise again as vampire and become Dresdan."

"Did it hurt?" she asked.

"I don't remember much about the transformation. He fed me his dreams and memories to divert my

Prelude

attention away from the discomfort. The change happened over a period of a few days. We are all fledgling vampires before we ever come into our own. The ascension process takes more than a few days."

"Ascension."

"We ascend through the blood, kind of like a hierarchy. Humans are at the bottom. And then we have blood slaves. On top of them, we have Donors."

"Wait...blood slaves and Donors."

Vicq nodded. "Yes, these are humans who willingly offer blood to Dresdan. Donors, of course, only belong to one Dresdan."

"What's next?"

"Fledglings are newly created vampires. They're like students and really don't become viable members of the Court until they've ascended to Soldier status. After becoming a Soldier, there are very few who will make it as Superiors. Superiors are as close to a Master vampire as many will become. Masters usually serve until death or permanent slumber."

"What are you?"

"I was a Superior to Master Zaket until Russo betrayed him. While he was in slumber, Russo took it upon himself to behead my Maker."

Her eyes widened. "Okay...that's harsh."

"I denounced all ties to Russo and what he stood for, so I am no longer a ranking member of the Court. I run with a circle of vampires called a coven."

"Coven?" she whispered.

"Yes, Elaina. Coven."

"What's it like being a Donor?"

He smiled. "I've never been one."

The way she pressed her full lips together stirred his libido. He was so close he could pick up on the imbalance in her blood as her mood changed from complacent to anxious.

"Do you have a Donor?"

"No, I've fed freely...up until now."

She licked her lips. "What do you mean, up until now?"

Prelude

"It means I've found my preferred blood type in you. All Dresdan have a preferred blood subtype. There are four main types that provide sustenance, whether we like the taste of it or not. Partaking of all four will provide a Dresdan a well-balanced diet. And then there are thousands of subgroups, but only one of those groups appeals to each Dresdan's appetite. When they find what that subgroup is, nothing else will ever compare. In fact, when a match like that occurs, a mating bond almost always follows. And even though I detect chemicals in your blood from the drugs you've been given, I can still tell that you were meant for me."

"I don't know what to say."

"I wanted you to know, but by no means am I trying to be pushy. I'm still coming to terms with the fact that I've found something a Dresdan can literally take decades—*centuries*—to find. And some Dresdan never find a mate with whom they can truly bond with."

She laughed nervously. "Do you understand what I am? A vampire killer. I've killed creatures just like you."

"Creatures?"

"Sorry...we were told—"

"Forget what your organization told you. Everything was a lie. Don't you see that now?"

Elaina didn't answer right away. She looked down at her open palms. "This is all so surreal. You tasted me once, maybe twice, and now you think my blood is your magic potion."

"It goes both ways, Elaina. You just don't know it yet, and you won't know it until I've shared mine with you," he said.

"But I'm only human."

"Yes, but that makes no difference. Humans have cravings, as well."

Her gaze rose to meet him. "Then give me your blood."

"Excuse me?"

"You said I would know if I tasted you. Prove it."

"You want to bite me?" He grinned.

Prelude

"No, I just want you to give me your blood from the vein," she said.

He laughed. "Doesn't quite work that way."

"Just slit your wrist and give it to me," she taunted.

He extended his arm out and turned his wrist over so that it was facing upward. "Go ahead, slit it."

She hesitated. "You're toying with me." She shot up, walked over to the mantle again, and turned her back to him.

"I assure you, I'm not."

"You are."

When she spun around again, he pulled her close and kissed her. Fuck it, she would probably slay him for it, but he just couldn't help himself.

***

When Elaina spun around to confront him, Vicq instantly embraced her and his lips descending onto hers. Blood raced through her veins and throbbed in her eardrums. She was nervous and excited all at once. Maybe a combination of both, but she knew what the consequences of her actions were.

His heated lips left a trail along her collarbone down to the plump cleavage peeking from the top of her fitted tee. His wicked tongue tasted the sensitive skin there.

"Vicq." Elaina grasped his arms tightly as he nuzzled her.

"You still have time to stop me," he whispered.

"I don't want you to stop." She arched her breasts toward him. She hadn't done this in so long. She wanted, needed it.

He exhaled as though he were relieved.

"If you want me so badly, take me," she said.

He lifted her top over her head with haste. Her bra fell down to the floor shortly after, freeing her breasts to his gaze. He lowered his head and took a hardened nipple between his lips. Cupping her back for support, he suckled gently. Each delicate tug caused a frenzy of

Prelude

lust to spread throughout her body. Her insides felt like they were on fire, heat rising within her like an inferno.

Vicq gently rolled a nipple between his fingers as he softly licked the other. The contrast—the roughness of his tongue, the softness of his lips, the smoothness of his fingertips, the urgency of his caresses—drove her absolutely insane. Another part of her demanded attention. His wicked tongue caused a heat wave at her core.

"I want to taste every inch of you, not just your blood."

They took turns tasting and savoring.

His fingertips slipped into the waistband of her jeans. He helped her pull them down her legs and then traced the lace edges of her panty line. The flesh between her legs ached so badly; she couldn't imagine why any women—blood slave or Donor—would want to endure such torture. Elaina cried out against his shoulder as his fingers circumvented her panties and dipped into her wet heat. He slid his fingers down into her folds, stroking her. Her knees buckled and she held onto his forearms for support.

Vicq mumbled something against her flesh that she didn't understand. His accent and the soft foreign words he whispered to her turned her brains to mush. When he spoke English again, he said, "You're hot for me." He used his body to urge her backwards until her back hit the wall. "I bet you taste just as sweet as your blood."

Elaina pushed her head against the wall and closed her eyes as his fingers stroked her outer lips. Immobilized, she couldn't even speak.

"May I?"

She sucked in her breath and nodded.

He lifted her in his arms, and just as he'd done to get them here, fled up two flights of stairs at the speed of light. She barely had time to catch her breath.

After shedding the rest of her garments, he stood over her and gazed down at her for what seemed like several minutes. His eyes traced over every curve of

Prelude

her body from head to toe. A never-ending caress. Sparks of red flickered in his eyes.

Vicq pulled his own shirt over his head, and her gaze immediately shifted to the ink-like symbol on his chest. Almost like a tattoo, but she knew the vampires were marked based on what breed they were. He unzipped his jeans, threw them aside, and then came down over her, slowly.

His heavy cock swept against her skin as he peppered her with kisses from head to toe. He brushed his cool fingertips against her skin, as if admiring the feel of her warm body against his own. When he dipped his tongue into the crevice of her navel, she gasped and grabbed a fistful of his hair. He laughed softly into her stomach and then moved lower and blew puffs of air on her belly.

"Vicq."

She anticipated what came next when his lips brushed her thigh. He kissed her sex once, twice...

"Turn over," he commanded.

"Vicq, I need..." She bit her lips. When she didn't obey him, he licked the inside of each thigh.

"Don't you like being teased?" he asked.

"Yes, but I need something now," she begged. She never begged.

"You need what?" He brought his hand over her sex and slid his fingers through her slit. "*Mierda*, you are so wet."

She squeezed her insides against his thick digit, as he pushed in and out of her. The walls of her sex gripped his fingers, and her clit pulsed rhythmically in harmony with his thrusts.

"Come," he whispered.

Her orgasm was near. So near, waiting on the edge. Elaina clutched the sheets when her convulsions began. Her orgasm burned through her like an erupting volcano.

Vicq grinned and then dipped his head again to place his lips to her clit.

She gasped and grabbed his hair. His strands

Prelude

felt like silk between her fingers. His tongue felt like heaven against her sex.

His tongue entered her, and he alternated between thrusting and licking. She showed him the rhythm she liked, holding her fingers against his scalp and lifting her hips off the bed to meet his lips. She came undone again, and this time her climax filtered through every cell in her body.

Vicq worked his way up her body gently, settling between her legs. He brushed the hair from her face and then kissed her forehead. His eyes burned red and his fangs had already descended.

Elaina didn't fear him. She craved him.

She wrapped her legs around his hips and arched upward.

He pushed himself into her sex one inch at a time. His cock felt just as good as his tongue inside of her, and when he started pumping, her body grew pliant beneath him and she gave herself over completely. Every stroke sent her further into ecstasy. She savored every one of his kisses.

He lifted her chin and nipped at the underside of her throat. His fangs scraped her neck gently, testing her readiness.

She dug her nails into his back, and he began to plunge with determination. He held his fangs against her neck. He was holding back. She could tell.

"Do it," she whispered against his hair and then threaded her fingers through his strands. "Is this what you want? Me as your Donor? Your personal sunshine?" She pulled his head in closer to her until she felt his lips against her throbbing vein.

"There's no going back, Elaina...once I do this..."

"I know," she said. "You'll crave my blood forever. That's what you meant earlier."

"Yes. I'll only crave yours."

"I want that..."

He sunk his fangs deeply into her neck, breaking through the skin with ease. She screamed. Another climax consumed her, but this time it felt different. No pain, only pleasure. He siphoned and drank her blood in the same slow driving rhythm that he took her sex. His release came as he was feeding from her. Streams of semen filled her the same way her blood had flooded his mouth. The feeding lasted minutes, but she would provide what he craved for as long as he craved it.

Vicq slipped his fangs from her vein and rested his face against her chest. "Elaina...my sunshine."

CHAPTER FOURTEEN

"Have you ever made another vampire?" Elaina asked.

They were seated on the grass at a river's edge under the moonlight. Vicq was resting back on a tree, while she leaned into his chest enjoying his embrace and the view. Her legs were stretched out with his and her head rested close to his heart. The sounds of nightlife and the rustling of the tree branches blended beautifully with the water rippling downstream.

"I've made many. Too many to count. Both while I was serving under the Court and about a dozen more after I fled," he said.

"What happens to vampires who flee from the Court?"

"It's a punishable offense to denounce ties to the Court. Most are captured and executed."

"This Court is always led by a Master vampire right? Is the one who betrayed your Maker the Master of the Dresdan Court now?"

Vicq's body tensed against her. "*Sí.*"

"If he wronged you and the Court by betraying another Dresdan, why can't he be removed as leader?" she asked.

"That's not how the Court is operated. If one manages to kill a Master, they reap everything. My Maker, Zaket, was also Russo's Maker."

"Are you the only one in your Court that hates Russo for betraying Zaket?"

"No, I'm not," he said. "There are dozens who denounced ties and fled. Some have already been captured, especially the ones who formed covens and tried to devise a plan to regain control of the Court and the Dresdan population."

"You're a member of a coven, right? Do you think Russo will come for you?"

"He has tried to bring me down countless times."

She placed her palms on the top of his hands and threaded her fingers with his. "Are you afraid?"

Prelude

"Of what?" he asked, his breath fanning her face.

"Of being executed?"

"No. Throughout the decades, a vampire gains the ability to subdue emotions, especially fear."

Elaina paused for a moment to meditate on his answer. "Fear allows us to feel our humanity. It's the emotion that reminds of us of just how vulnerable we are. It's the emotion that we feel right before we're faced with what limits us and raises doubt in our hearts."

"*Precisamente.* Fear is what happens when we risk losing something."

"Is there nothing in your life worth keeping?" she asked, turning her head slightly eager for his answer.

"There is now." He lifted her hair from her shoulders and pressed his lips to her neck. *"Te adoro... mi rayo de sol."*

A small gasp pushed passed her lips when she felt the cool point of his fangs testing the delicate skin on the back of her neck. She closed her eyes and waited for the bite, which he seemed to delay on purpose.

"*Voy a asesinar a los que te marcó,*" he whispered into her skin.

"You'll have to teach me this language," she replied, not understanding a word he spoke.

"Through the blood. In due time."

"When will you give me your blood?" she asked.

"I want to make sure you really want it before I do that," he replied. "You won't be the same once I do. It's only fair that I introduce you to who I really am. Once you take my blood, you will become more acquainted with my dark side but I want you to know who I am as it now stands."

"Are you also afraid that I will no longer be *el sol* if you give me your blood?"

"*Siempre serás mi sol.* Always."

She smiled. "*Marcó…?* What does it mean?"

"Marcado. *Voy a asesinar a los que te marcó,*" he told her. "It means that I'll murder those who have marked you."

Remembering the mark of the District burned into

Prelude

the flesh on the back of her neck, she slid her palm up to caress it. "This will never disappear, will it?"

Vicq kissed her fingers. "It will...if you want it to."

"I do." Elaina turned around to face him, placed her thighs on either side of his, and straddled him. She initiated a kiss that lasted for several minutes. Before long, her hips were moving in tandem to the thrusts of his pelvis. She wanted him and he sensed it. Vicq brought her to stand and paid great attention as she rid herself of her boots and leather jumpsuit. He shed his clothes within a matter of seconds. Starting at her shoulders, he rained kisses all over her skin, venturing downward until his head was level with the apex of her thighs. He caressed her backside and pleasured her sex with his lips and tongue as he knelt on the ground before her.

Elaina was already wet by the time she led him back down to a seating position on the ground. She straddled him again, sliding her sex down over his cock until the length of him was buried to the hilt inside of her. Wrapping her arms around his head, she embraced him with her fingers tangled through his silky black hair. As she rode him, she bared her neck, offering her vampire lover the thickest part of her vein. This time, he accepted without hesitation. Her blood pulsed into his mouth at the same tempo as her hips moved sensuously over him.

She reached her first peak, moaning softly into his hair. "Vicq..."

He extracted his fangs and exhaled and inhaled harshly to catch his breath. It wasn't long before he descended on her again for another taste.

Elaina rode Vicq through midnight just like that, under the stars and under the moonlight. Her adrenaline levels rose with every bite he delivered and every breath she took. When he reached his orgasm, sheer unrelenting pleasure barreled through her. He was like a drug, better than any drug. Her addiction for Vicq had grown in such a short time. This craving instilled a need so great that she just might long for his touch forever with the knowledge that Vicq offered eternal satisfaction.

CHAPTER FIFTEEN

❖

"Is it good?" Vicq asked, eyeing her from across the small table.

They were seated at a small twenty-four-hour diner in a town out in the middle of nowhere. Vicq had been watching her eat for almost fifteen minutes. She was on her second serving of scrambled eggs and protein pancakes.

She nodded, swallowed, and chugged down some ice-cold water. "I haven't been this hungry in a very long time."

"Do you know why that is?" he asked.

She frowned at him. "I'm not that different from you, ya know? I'm hungry because I need sustenance… the same way you need blood." She added the last part with her tone lowered.

Although it was 2AM, there were a few truckers that had stopped in and were seated at nearby tables.

"A few days of me feeding from you will do that," Vicq said.

He fumbled with the basket of toast set out in front of him. He hadn't even pretended to be eating. He just sat there, watching her. Well, that was fine with Elaina. When it came to food and eating, she wasn't shy. If she didn't burn as many calories as she ate on a daily basis, she'd probably have more curves where she'd always wanted them to be.

"Then I conclude that having a Donor is costing you more than you expected." She held up the guest bill and glanced at the double digit cost of her meal.

He laughed. "I wouldn't have it any other way. I want you to be well fed."

"What are our plans for tonight? As much as I love the things we do in the dark in your bedroom, I'd love to play some other ways, too."

His eyebrow rose as he assessed her. "Have any ideas?"

"You said you'd show me how to easily track a rogue."

Prelude

"I did, didn't I? What if I say I don't want my woman around danger?"

She smiled. "Understood, but don't ever forget how we first met. I wasn't wearing a frilly dress, selling cupcakes after Sunday school then, was I? I don't mind getting my hands dirty."

"Oh, don't I know it." He grinned.

"So, is that a deal? You show me how to track a rogue without being sensed, and I might let you bite my neck again." She winked.

Vicq narrowed his gaze. "I'll think about it."

Elaina shrugged. "Think all you want, but while time's a wastin', you'll go hungry."

***

"We've got a few more hours until all the rogues are likely to retreat to their slumbering places, so you're in luck," Vicq said as they reached his motorcycle.

Elaina stuffed her satchel into the tail box. "Do

they slumber sooner because they're not as strong as Dresdan?"

"That's part of the reason. They also slumber often because they're still considered fledging." He handed her a helmet.

"Thanks." She closed the gap between them, pressing her body against his to kiss his lips.

Vicq responded as he always did, kissing her back firmly, but gently. And what had started as a long, sensual kissing session became a series of short kisses between panting.

"Hmmmm," she moaned as he cupped and gently kneaded her ass. "I think maybe we should finish this first."

"Of course, I'm ready whenever you are." He demonstrated by pressing the hard length of his cock against her belly and scraping his fangs across her neck.

Elaina wanted both his cock and his fangs inside of her. This craving for him seemed never ending, and

Prelude

she had yet to take any of his blood. She could only imagine what the first taste of his blood would have her doing.

She—

Her train of thought was cut off and a sharp object splintered through her shoulder. The impact was so sudden that it knocked the wind right out of her. Her knees gave out instantly and she slumped against Vicq.

Her vision went in and out as a pain so great it almost made her black out traveled through her rapidly.

"No..." Vicq screamed.

Just before her eyes rolled back into her head, she saw the shooter on the roof with a crossbow. A District 5 tracker had just shot her with a poisoned arrow. She couldn't move. It was as if everything had frozen in time.

So this was death...

CHAPTER SIXTEEN

❖

"Elaina, please...open your mouth and take more." A man was talking to her. Vicq.

"Where am I?" She inhaled deeply and smelled nothing but Earth and a metallic scent. Her blood. She was on the ground, eyes looking upward toward the dusky sky. It was dawn.

There was so much pain, and she just wanted to go back to sleep.

Vicq shook her. "Elaina...quick! I'm being trailed."

"What are you talking about?" She licked her dry lips and tasted blood. Vicq's blood.

"Dozens, Elaina. I can't fight them all now. You kept passing out and I had to feed you. Keep drinking."

Her instincts told her to take what her body needed, and she parted her lips. Vicq's ancient blood flowed like lava down her throat.

He grabbed her against his chest and squeezed

tightly. "Fuck! I can't even shift away from here."

"What happened?" Elaina was slowly regaining her eyesight.

"You were shot with a crossbow. I pulled it out. The more blood you lost, the more I kept losing you."

"You drained yourself, didn't you?" she asked and tried to lift herself up.

"Don't try to get up. The blood is helping you heal internally. It may take a couple of days. Elaina. Listen to me..." He looked over his shoulder. "I've been trailed. I shifted us here, but it's likely that dozens of Soldiers are on to me. I'm too far away from any of my coven members to send a call out for help."

"What does that mean?" She grabbed his arm, and realized that she was weaker than she'd thought.

"You're going to stay here, behind this bus. Under no circumstances are you to reveal your location. Understood?"

Elaina looked around and realized that they were on the ground near a deserted building in a parking

Prelude

lot filled with buses that looked like they hadn't been maintained in months.

"Who's after you?" she asked.

"I smell Dresdan blood. These are no rogues. No one would dare trail me unless ordered to."

"Russo...?"

He nodded. "I have to leave, Elaina. I can't pull you into this."

"Can you just fight them off?" she urged.

"It's an option, but I sensed too many and I'm completely drained."

"Damn it, Vicq. I wish I was strong enough to help you."

"You have my blood and you'll be strong enough soon, sunshine."

He kissed her forehead and fled the area.

Elaina bit back a curse and remained huddled near the bus. Moments later, a sea of thick mist clouded the parking lot. Not five minutes after that, the mist was gone and the first rays of sunshine pooled over

Elaina's body.

    She shielded her eyes with her forearm.

    The sunshine was the last thing she wanted right now.

CHAPTER SEVENTEEN

❖

Shit.

Dozens of Dresdan Soldiers began to materialize around Vicq, swarming him like flies, and pouncing around like rabid, hungry gutter rats in their excitement over finally catching up to him. They'd trailed his blood essence here while he was busy helping rid Elaina's body of the poison. The lethal does could have killed her, so Vicq had literally drained himself saving her. He estimated that he was still standing because of what little blood remained within his veins.

Yet still, he tried to fold away again, but he was just too weak to do anything.

He tried to focus on the entities unfolding in front of him, but he struggled to stay conscious. His body was trying to pull him into slumber but he tried to remain standing.

A Superior vampire shrugged his way out from the

crowd of vampires. "Well, well, well...what happened to you? Did a human shoot you? You're bleeding out all over the place. We trailed your essence from miles away."

Vicq opened his mouth to speak, but nothing came out. He swayed from left to right, fading in and out of consciousness.

The Superior laughed. "My...you're drained nearly dry."

Vicq's knees buckled, but yet he struggled to stand. His body fought to lure him into slumber. He was too weak to shift away to his basement. That wasn't even an option at this point. He would never reveal his place of slumber to any enemy.

The rising sun burned his shoulders. The UV rays affected him more than it did the Soldiers waiting to strike and the Superior that led them.

"It's too bad you can't put up a fight. Russo told me I'd have so much fun bringing you down," the Superior continued.

Prelude

Vicq swallowed hard, mustering all of the strength he had left within. "Fuck you. Fuck Russo."

The Superior lunged. Before Vicq could dart out of the vampire's path, someone struck him on the head with an object. He saw blackness just before the full force of sunshine hit him.

CHAPTER EIGHTEEN

❖

A biting pang of hunger ripped through Vicq's belly causing him to rise abruptly. He dragged himself up off the concrete floor, pulling at the heavy chains binding his arms and legs to the ground. Judging from how much he'd recovered, Vicq estimated that he'd slept for half a day.

He was locked in some kind of dungeon and enclosed in a cell no bigger than the size of the master bathroom at his manor. There were others around him in the other cells. He could smell them, but from his position in the cell, he couldn't see them. Some of them were even human, probably Blood Slaves who had defied orders.

Before Vicq could investigate any further, three vampires instantly materialized before him. One of them was Russo—the traitorous Dresdan he hadn't seen in years. Vicq wanted to stand because he refused to bow to Russo, but the chains were pulled taut limiting his ability to rise.

"Hello Vicq," Russo rasped. "My blood brother."

"You are no brother of mine," Vicq said between clenched teeth, finally lifting his gaze to meet Russo's.

Russo's eyes were pitch black, almost the same color as the iron cells surrounding them. He looked the exact same, sporting thick long blond almost golden hair that flowed down his back. He was tall and slender, but his smaller size had never been mistaken for weakness. And he was known for his morally deficient ways and ability to flip alter egos at any moment. His looks disgusted Vicq, but women loved him. Both human and vampire alike. It was said that he had dozens of blood slaves to quench his thirst.

"No? But we share the same Maker."

"A Maker who you betrayed."

Russo sucked his cheeks in and narrowed his gaze. "Why is putting one out of one's misery called betrayal?"

Prelude

"It wasn't your call. If he wanted a final death, he would have done it himself."

Russo tucked in his upper lip and shook his head. "But when? He was leading us all down a hopeless path! We were being slaughtered left and right by an agency known as *District* and blamed for the faulty actions of rogues and other vampire clans. We were in a era of chaos. It was time to fight back and he didn't want to fight. He was too weak to lead us."

"As you are." Vicq's voice rose to match Russo's. "Your rage against humans has spread to your followers to the point where they don't even think twice about lashing out and murdering innocents for blood. We are not rogues. We are Dresdan. And until this Court stops condoning the senseless acts of violence, I will have nothing to do with it."

Russo smirked. "I didn't give you a choice."

"I never asked you for one. I'll never serve under you."

Russo scoffs and glanced back and forth between

the two vampires on either side of him. "Then you shall die. You shall be the prime example of what happens to those who defy my orders and give me a bad name inside and outside of the Court. You shall burn." Russo pointed to the ceiling.

Vicq glanced up and noted the shaded filter over an opening in the ceiling. He needed no one to tell him that what awaiting above was the burning rays of the sun.

"Anything else you wish to say?" Russo asked.

Vicq fixed his gaze directly on his enemy. "Getting rid of me won't end this. You will fail."

"Then I'll fail until I succeed." Russo turned to the vampire on his left. "Unsheathe your knife and shave his head. Open the top door and let him burn. You two will stand guard today over this cell. You will rotate until he is gone." Russo chuckled and turned to leave. "You better feed well on your breaks. This one is strong. We've starved him, yet he still lives. It could be weeks before he crumbles up and dies."

CHAPTER NINETEEN

❖

Elaina used the box cutter to slice through another box with some of her belongings. She tried to remember where she had put stuff since leaving her parents' home, but her memory was all a blur. Plus, she fought to hold back the tears that were flooding her eyes. She refused to cry. Not now. Later she might, but time wasn't on her side.

Something tapped on the outside of the storage unit and she turned her attention in that direction, thinking it was the clerk who'd given her the keys, telling her that her time was up. But no one was there.

Elaina glanced down at her wristwatch and noted that the place had closed five minutes ago—6PM—so it had been nice of the old lady up front to let her grab some things while she closed up.

She grabbed a couple of maps that her dad had given her and hastily stuffed them into one of the duffle bags.

"Who's there?" Elaina spun around when she heard the same tapping noise. "I know you're there. I can smell you. Come out, before I come to you," she warned.

A female laughed and then fully materialized by the wall. "Vicq did say you were brazen."

Elaina rose at the mention of Vicq's name. "Who are you?"

The woman flashed her fangs. "Does it matter?"

"How do you know Vicq?"

"I run with him. He's the leader of my coven," the female said.

"Do you know where he was taken?" Elaina urged. "I need to find him."

The female shook her head. "We got word that he was taken in to face Russo. I wouldn't advise you to try and find him. You don't know what you're up against."

Elaina frowned. "There's only one way to find out."

"He betrayed the Court and that's why he was

Prelude

taken in. You're better off leaving him alone. You carry a tracker's mark. The mark of that filthy organization. Another reason why you shouldn't go after him. They'd rip you to shreds...after draining you, of course."

"They'd have to catch me first."

"Don't be a stupid woman. All you humans are, thinking you can defy the odds. Do you think you have a chance against hundreds of Russo's Soldiers? Vicq didn't...and surely you don't. It's gotten to the point where those in my coven who were made by him can't even detect his blood presence anymore. Protect yourself. Was his saving you in vain? Do you want to die?"

"I'm not afraid of dying."

"Tell me what happened when he was taken in," she demanded.

Elaina opened her mouth to speak, but regret rose in her throat. She shook her head. "I..."

"Give me your wrist."

She eyed the vampiress incredulously, but felt

guilt for what happened to Vicq when he risked everything to save her. She extended her arm, wrist up, and closed her eyes.

The vampiress didn't hesitate as she grabbed her hand and sunk her fangs through the thickest vein. She fed for a few minutes and then pushed Elaina's arm aside. She had a sour expression on her face before she said, "We could have saved Vicq, but instead, he got caught while he was with you. Trying to save you after those people you aligned yourself with shot you. You caused this. Now, because of you, he will be executed."

Elaina grimaced, trying to bottle up her agony.

"I honored Vicq," she continued. "I could kill you for this. The only reason I have second thoughts is because of what I saw through your blood. He cared deeply for you."

"I cared for him too," Elaina replied.

"I was once like you," the female said. "Wanting to take on the world and seek revenge against those who wronged me and my family. And now I'm no longer

Prelude

human."

"No longer human, but at least you can still take revenge."

She folded her arms across her chest. "I urge you not to try anything stupid. There's no other vampire you should trust after this. Not even me. I came to kill you. My coven members never trusted you, but Vicq did. I see it now in your blood. We warned him to stay away from you. Why do you think he never brought you near us, huh?"

Those words hurt Elaina, and she swallowed down her pride. It confirmed her fate. Even though she could technically bond with Vicq, it would have never worked. She was marked as an enemy. He was leader of his coven. How could he lead his followers if he bonded with an ex-District 5 member?

"Ah...those human emotions will surface every time," the vampiress teased. "You worry about him, don't you? Don't feel bad. Good things never last. Suck it up and get on with your life, huh?"

Elaina slid the tip of her tongue against her top row of teeth. Hunger gnawed at her gut. The aftertaste of Vicq's blood still filled her memories. "Maybe I will."

"You should...its all a matter of life or death," were the vampiress' last words before she disappeared.

Elaina decided to heed the warning this time.

By the next morning, she was already on a train headed west. Exactly where she would end up, only time would tell.

EPILOGUE

❖

The prison guard's keys rattled as he made a pit stop next to Vicq's cell.

Vicq didn't even bother to lift his head. Even if he tried, he doubted he could. He had no strength and not much blood left within him. Most of his skin had been burned away until only raw flesh remained. He didn't even know what day it was or how many days had passed since he met the sun. Two days? Five days? A week? Fuck, it felt like he'd been burning in this cell forever.

"Are you dead yet?" the guard asked.

"Fuck you," Vicq grumbled.

"You're the one who's fucked now." The guard chuckled. "You got a little break yesterday. Today's luminous power is expected to be much higher. Tell me, traitor, are you ready for more sunshine?"

Death by sunshine. Who would have known that

this was how his fate would unfold? He had no regrets. He'd do it again to protect Elaina—*mi sol, mi amor.*

About the Author

Amber Ella Monroe pens seductive tales of paranormal romance. She also writes contemporary romance as Ambrielle Kirk. As a child, she never really dreamed of being an author. It was a destined path that chose her. Now she writes with her readers in mind, but the characters, of course, dictate the outcome.

Visit her website at http://amberellabooks.com if you enjoy romance with an edgier side or subscribe to her newsletter at http://smarturl.it/amberellas-list.

Made in the USA
Lexington, KY
19 April 2016